FEELINGS OF POWER

INITIATION

T.J. Genesis

mill city press,
minneapolis

Copyright © 2016 by T.J. Genesis

MILL CITY PRESS

Mill City Press, Inc.
322 First Avenue N, 5th floor
Minneapolis, MN 55401
612.455.2293
www.millcitypublishing.com

All rights reserved. No part of this publication may be reproduced, stored in a retrieval system, or transmitted, in any form or by any means, electronic, mechanical, photocopying, recording, or otherwise, without the prior written permission of the author.

ISBN-13: 978-1-63505-139-1
LCCN: 2016904327

Cover Design by Emily Keenan
Typeset by Mary Ross

Printed in the United States of America

To all the crazy characters in my life
who made this possible.

CHAPTER 1

We enter an interrogation room with a young man handcuffed in his chair. It is a room he has been in before. He is also well acquainted with the small man sitting across the table with him.

Man: So Blake, you know why I brought you in here?
Blake: Because you don't like the people I hang out with?

Frustration followed by joy. Interesting.

The man smiles and throws a folder on the desk. Blake raises his restrained hands onto the metal table and lifts it open. Multiple pictures of graffiti litter the inside of the manila folder.

Blake: Street art, what's your point?

Frustration.

Man: Maybe you wouldn't think of it as art if you had to clean it up.
Blake: Why would I be cleaning it?
Man: You and your friends are the ones who put it there.
Blake: When?
Man: Last night.
Blake: Wasn't me.
Man: I know it was.
Blake: You are very confident today Joel. I imagine you have another folder filled with pictures of me and my friends doing this.

Irritation.

Joel's lip twitches as he pulls the folder back to him. He stares intently into Blake's blue eyes.

Joel: So you didn't do it?
Blake: No I did not.
Joel: Do you know who did?
Blake: Can't say I do.

Anger.

Joel whips the folder into the wall then walks out of the room. Blake looks sideways at the window. The bright sunlight coming in is starting to acquire an orange hue.

Disappointment. Laura.

A woman walks into the room. She is wearing a nice blue overcoat that matches her blue skirt. Her long

Chapter 1

brown hair is tied into a professional ponytail. Blake looks into her kind brown eyes and smiles.

Blake: Hi Laura.
Laura: Don't you smile at me.
Blake: What? You know Joel is full of it.
Laura: He might be, you do hang out with some less than desirable people.
Blake: Depends what you consider desirable traits.
Laura: Grand theft auto, property damage, loitering, and assault are not good traits.
Blake: I didn't know all that.
Laura: Why do you hang out with these kids?
Blake: They don't lie to me.
Laura: Apparently they don't tell you everything either.
Blake: Apparently.
Laura: Did you mark those walls?
Blake: No.

Joy.

Laura doesn't even crack a grin.

Laura: Good.
Blake: Can I go?
Laura: I'll be taking you home.
Blake: I can walk on my own.
Laura: Oh I know, I just want to make sure I know where you go.
Blake: Don't trust me?
Laura: No, I don't trust the choices you make.
Blake: Isn't that the same thing?
Laura: No.

She takes off his handcuffs and they walk out to her car.

Blake: Do I have to sit in the back?

Irritation.

Laura: You want to?
Blake: Nope, sorry.

The car is an old Crown Vic but it looks as if it just came off the lot. They get in the car and go. Blake stares off into the distance.

Laura: I'm worried about you Blake.
Blake: I know.
Laura: Is there any way you can hang out with people that aren't trouble?
Blake: I'll try.
Laura: I don't want to see you for like two weeks.
Blake: That's hurtful.
Laura: You can come visit with me, but don't be brought in.
Blake: Ok.

They stop in front of a large brick building with two garage doors facing them. A muscular man is standing outside leaning against the building. He has sandy blonde hair. His t-shirt is torn and covered in oil, so are his jeans. Laura gets out of the vehicle.

Laura: What's up Rick?
Rick: Not much, there a reason you're bringing my kid home?

Chapter 1

Laura: He was walking and I was heading this way.
Rick: It isn't because Joel picked him up earlier?
Laura: Nope, not his time.

Joy.

Rick: Good.

Blake smiles at Laura and walks up to Rick.

Rick: She's way too nice to you.
Blake: I completely agree.
Rick: Ready.
Blake: Always.

Intense rage.

Blake: Watch out.

Blake and Rick step to the side. *TUNG!* Something hits the nearest garage door with force.

Laura: What was that!?
Rick: Looks like Uncle Jeff will be making dinner tonight.
Blake: Yep.
Rick: Good, he's better at it anyway.
Laura: Well I'm going to head out. I better not get a call back here.
Rick: He'll be fine, probably just a rusty bolt.

Blake and Rick walk into a side door and into the garage. A thin man in overalls is sitting with his hands in his short black hair.

Feelings of Power

Rick: Sup.
Jeff: Bolt won't come off.
Rick: Figured. What you going to do?
Jeff: I'll get the big wrench.
Rick: Supper time?
Jeff: Yeah, what sounds good?
Blake: Burgers?
Jeff: Deal.

Jeff walks up to the sink and washes his hands.

Rick: Looks like you're bleeding.
Jeff: Dang, when did that happen?
Blake: Looks pretty deep.
Jeff: Good thing I'm done for today or I'd have to put a mandage on it.

Jeff pulls some gauze out of a cupboard and wraps his hand up. They walk into the back of the garage together. Upon opening the door, a very large tile floor comes into view. It leads into a kitchen and large living room. Jeff takes off his overalls and hangs them on the coat rack. Jeff walks up to the freezer and pulls out a slab of cheese. *Tatunk!* He drops it on the counter.

Jeff: So, who's running to the store?
Blake: I will.

Rick pulls out his wallet and hands Blake a twenty dollar bill.

Rick: I want a majority of my change back.
Blake: (Smiles) Ok.

Chapter 1

Blake runs out the front door.

I really should do better. People lie for a reason, it's not their fault I'm a freak.

Tingles ripple through his entire body.

Walk towards the feeling or away from it?

He heads toward the odd feeling. It is coming from a large group trees in the park. The park itself is very large, but often only occupied in the daytime.

Oh great, the most secluded part. Fear? I should run away.

He moves closer to the trees.

Hunger.

A large dog jumps out of the trees. It is six feet tall with dark-red eyes. Its huge fangs have a blood-like liquid dripping off of them. Blake steps forward and the dog begins to growl.

Anger.

Blake steps back and the dog steps forward.

Anticipation. You're watching me aren't you?

The dog walks towards him with its mouth open. Blake clenches his fists.

Feelings of Power

Stress.

The dog lunges at him. Blake effortlessly moves to the side.

Disappointment. Anger.

Blake: That last one isn't from you.

Blake searches around.

Stress.

The dog lunges again. Blake ducks down and picks up a stick. The dog lands behind him.

Disappointment, Frustration, and Anger. You're getting orders from someone, are you?

Blake knocks a rock into the bushes. *Thunk!*

Tree.

He knocks two more rocks into the bushes. *Thunk! Thud!*

Pain and Anger.

The dog grazes him and knocks him on the ground, hard.

Blake: It would be real nice if you sat down.

Chapter 1

The dog sits.

Blake: (nods) Good boy.

The dog stands back up and growls.

Blake: Well it was a nice gesture.

Blake runs off into the bushes. He swings wildly with the stick.

Anger. Anger. Anger. Fear.

Thwack! The stick connects with something soft.

Pain. Gotcha!

Squish! The dog sinks its teeth into Blake's shoulder. A small, long-haired, body falls to the ground. The dog runs over to check on the fallen figure. Dark-purple goop oozes out of its head. Long cone-like nails slither out of the blood-red hair. The figure pushes itself upward. *Squish!* It cuts the dog along the side.

Blake: Well miss, I can say you didn't age well.

Hate.

It waves its nails at Blake. The dog growls and walks towards him. He holds his shoulder. Blood is running down it. He points at the old woman.

Blake: I'm way nicer to you than she is. I haven't hit you once and you're attacking me. If I was you, I would bite her.

The dog turns and growls at her. She waves her hand. The dog turns its attention back at Blake. Blake's shoulder burns. He winces.

Blake: Get her!

The dog turns and jumps at the old woman. *Squish!* Its fangs sink deeply into her throat. *Screeeeee!* A scream rips through Blake's ears. He covers his ears and falls to his knees. The dog walks over and whimpers at Blake. It licks his shoulder. The dog's side is cut very deeply. Blake presses his forehead to the dog's forehead.

Blake: It's alright buddy. You were just following orders. You're hurt worse than me anyhow.

The dog begins to growl.

Don't stop listening to me now bud. Anger.

Blake looks up. The dog is looking off into the distance. Lights are rapidly approaching.

Not growling at me, that's helpful.

Blake: Get out of here.

The dog runs off. Everything shrinks into darkness.

Chapter 1

Worry. Sadness. Worry. Anger. Sadness. Worry. Anger. Anger. Sadness. Anxiety. Frustration.

Blake awakes and lunges up clutching his head.

Surprise. Surprise.

He takes multiple deep breaths and tries to take in the room around him. It appears to be a small hospital room with a single bed. An attractive woman is standing next to him with her hands on his shoulder. She has tan skin and long brown hair. She is very focused on the wound on Blake's shoulder. He does his best not to look at her cleavage by looking up at the ceiling.

Woman: Hey.

Blake looks down and looks her in the eye. Her brown eyes almost seem to sparkle.

Blake: Hi.
Woman: (Smiles) You look a lot better than you did when you came in here.
Blake: I feel great.

Happiness.

Woman: (Smiles) Then my work is done here.
Voice: Thank you Lisa.
Lisa: You are welcome.

As the woman walks out, Blake looks over to see a man in a suit sitting in the hospital chair. He has blonde spiky hair. Blake can see his blue eyes very clearly through his hands that appear to be praying. After seeing him, he spots a young girl leaning up against the wall. She has long black and red hair that covers her face. She is also wearing a suit, but a skirt instead of pants. Her white tights and black dress shoes almost make her look like a schoolgirl. She has her arms tucked behind her making it so none of her skin is showing. She looks up at him and reveals her pale skin and green eyes. They make eye contact. The muffled sound of a woman screaming fills his ears. Tears stream down his face.

Sadness.

The girl walks over and hugs him. His entire body feels like it was dipped in water that was just a little too hot.

Man: So much for feeling great.

The girl lets go of Blake and walks out of the room. Blake can feel her sadness through the door.

Blake: Sorry I don't know what that was. I'm alright now.
Man: That's good. What happened just now?
Blake: Like I said, I'm not sure.
Man: Ok.

The man stands up and walks to the foot of the bed. He pulls out the clip board and looks it over.

Chapter 1

Man: It doesn't state here that you had any head injuries, so I was curious why you grabbed your head when you woke up.
Blake: Just a headache.

Annoyance.

Man: Why don't you tell me what happened?
Blake: I went to pick up hamburger and woke up here.
Man: You don't remember anything besides that?
Blake: Nope.
Man: You're not a fan of authority are you?
Blake: Nope.

The man walks over to Blake and stands above him.

Man: I have speculation of what happened in that park, and you are not at fault for anything, but I need to know I am right.
Blake: Tell me what you think?

Amusement. Not from him though. Must be on the other side of the door.

Man: Let's see if we can jog your memory.

Pain. Sadness. Pain. Anger. Sadness. Uh oh.

Blake presses his right hand to the side of his head. The man grabs a chair and pulls it to the side of the bed. He crosses his arms.

Blake: Tell me what you know officer.

Feelings of Power

Man: My name is Grant. We found you unconscious in Granite Park. Your shoulder appears as though it was bitten by a dog.
Blake: Not triggering anything.
Grant: You were a few feet away from a dead body.

Sadness. Anger. Anger. Pain. Annoyance. Time to get out of here.

Blake removes his hand from his head and grips the blanket on top of him.

Grant: What's up?

Window isn't an option. Looks like it's time to take the door.

Woosh! Blake throws the blanket over Grant and bolts for the door. He makes it into the hallway.

Surprise. Anger. Joy. Pain. Pain. Anger. Sadness. Anxiety.

He falls to his hands and knees. The world begins to spin.

Wasn't quick enough.

Grant: You didn't make it far.
Blake: Get me out of here!

Blake gets the feeling of being lifted up and moved. Blake's vision returns to normal. He is in the backseat of a leather interior vehicle.

Chapter 1

Grant: (From the driver's seat) Better?
Blake: Yes thank you.
Grant: Ready to start telling me what's going on?
Blake: I went to go get hamburger. I felt something in the park. I walked towards it. Turned out to be some evil looking dog and a crazy woman. The dog bit me and killed her. I woke up.

Surprise. Surprise.

Girl's voice: You felt the portal open?

Blake jumps at the sudden noise. The girl in the schoolgirl outfit is sitting next to him in the backseat.

Blake: Yes?
Grant: The dog bit the old woman?
Blake: Right in the neck.

Confusion. Surprise.

Grant: You have any idea what's going on?
Blake: Nope.
Grant: I'll tell you what I can. The old woman was what we call a "handler". They control demonic pets. The pet you dealt with has been with her since it was born.
Blake: Poor thing.
Grant: The dog?
Blake: Yeah, she was pretty mean to him.
Grant: Typical, a handler has one-hundred percent control over the pet, so they usually take out their frustrations on the pets.
Blake: She didn't have full control over this one.

Grant: Obviously, which is unheard of.
Girl: What did the portal feel like?
Grant: You ever felt anything like it before?
Blake: No, I can feel others people's feelings, but they've never been like that.

Confusion.

Grant: Other people's feelings?
Blake: Yes. Like you just felt confused.

Surprise.

Blake: And surprised.
Grant: Quite a talent.
Blake: Normally, yes.
Grant: Except when you're in a hospital full of negative emotion.
Blake: Bingo. Thank you by the way.
Grant: For getting you out of there?
Blake: That and not asking any stupid questions while I was on the floor.

Amusement. Joy.

Grant: You're welcome. That why you've been so forthcoming with information now?
Blake: Yeah. Oh and thank you for pulling me from the park.
Grant: It's what we do.

Blake jumps.

Chapter 1

Blake: My dad is probably worried sick about me!
Grant: Well buckle up and I'll take you home.

They buckle and head towards Blake's house.

Girl: What is it like, feeling other people's emotions?

Blake looks over to see the girl looking at him. His entire body tingles. She is by far the most beautiful woman he has ever seen. Her face looks innocent with a touch of pain. His heart races. There is something eerily familiar about her. Blake holds out his hand.

Why should I know you? What was that screaming?

Blake: I'm Blake, sorry for the sadness earlier.
Girl: I'm Danielle. I understand, you've been through quite an ordeal.
Blake: It makes it hard to trust people, to answer your question.
Danielle: Why is that?
Blake: People hide how they feel more than anything. When I can see that, it's hard not to get a little annoyed.
Danielle: People have their reasons.
Blake: Yeah, I just hope they would trust me enough to tell me.
Danielle: They don't trust you, so you don't trust them.
Blake: Pretty much.

The vehicle stops.

Grant: We're here.
Blake: Thanks. How did you know where I lived?

Grant: Nurse ID'd you and I got all your info.

Blake unbuckles, opens the door, and steps out of the vehicle.

Grant: Stay safe out there.
Blake: Well let's just hope the freaky stuff stays away from me from now on.
Danielle: Don't think you can handle it?
Blake: If it keeps bringing you around, I welcome it with open arms.

Amusement. Embarrassment.

Danielle blushes. Blake places his right arm over his chest and bows.

Blake: Until we meet again.
Rick: Blake!

Blake turns and is greeted by his father's strong embrace. Blake feels a twinge of pain in his shoulder, but nothing he can't shake off.

Rick: What happened?

A car door opens and closes. Grant walks up to Dad with his hand out.

Grant: Hello sir, my name is Grant.

Fear!

Chapter 1

Thunk! A block of ice appears next to Grant's face. A metal marble resides in the middle of the ice.

Surprise. Anger. Anger. Surprise. Surprise. Surprise. Amusement.

Grant: If you could get in the house sir, it would be appreciated.

Blake looks to the street and sees two boys standing there. Both have a lanky build but one is about a foot taller than the other. The taller boy is tossing a marble up and down in his right hand. The shorter one is carrying two long poles with hooks on the end. Both of their faces are covered by scarfs.

Taller boy: Guess I shouldn't expect anything less from an agent of S.T.A.T.E.
Grant: Who are you and what do you want?

Pride. That's really close!

Blake's right fist connects with another assailant who appears right next to Grant. The assailant falls to the ground with both hands over their face. *Thud!* They land the ground hard.

Third assailant: You're going to...

Fear.

A fanged snout appears over the third assailants face. *Drip!* Blood drips onto their bandaged face. They roll out and jump over to the other two standing there.

Anger.

Taller boy: You alright Monique.
Third assailant: There is no way he could've known I was going to be there.
Shorter boy: His fist was heading to you before you got there.
Monique: What!? That's not possible Steve.
Taller boy: I saw it too. Looks like you'll have to try harder.
Monique: You guys better not be messing with me!

Blake looks at the dog that was standing over Monique. Large partially healed wounds occupy his side.

Blake: How did you get here?

The dog sits and wags its tail. Blake pats it on the head.

Blake: Thanks for the backup.
Grant: This the one from the park?
Blake: That's him.

Danielle steps out of the vehicle. A white glow wraps around her right hand. A small decorated hammer appears. Grant and Blake walk over to her. The dog stands next to Blake. Excitement fills the air. Blake's body tingles and the pain in his left shoulder completely vanishes.

Grant: What do you want?
Taller boy: That's not really your concern.

Chapter 1

The taller boy whips three marbles. They bounce erratically, but with considerable force. The odd thing is, they are moving in slow motion. Blake walks up and snatches them out the air.

Anger. Surprise. Surprise. How am I doing this!?

Steve: No way!
Taller boy: That's not possible.
Monique: I got him.

Two poles slide out of Monique's sleeves and she twists them together into a staff. Blake looks at the marbles in his hand. Lines appear from them and go off in thousands of directions. He throws the marbles as hard as he can. They bounce erratically and two of them hit Monique in each shoulder. She is thrown off balance. The dog jumps up and rips the staff out of her hands. The taller boy catches the third marble. *Thud!* Monique falls to the ground. The dog brings her staff to Blake. Blake grabs it with his right hand. The taller boy walks up and picks up Monique.

Taller boy: We'll be back.
Steve: I got him.

Fear. That makes two of us Steve.

Steve and Blake square off. Blake tightens his grip. Hundreds of images fill his head. They are all of faceless people wielding bo staffs. Steve jumps up and Blake catches both hooks.

Surprise.

The dog grabs Steve by the back of the shirt and throws him into his allies.

Taller boy: Ok we're done.
Steve: I'm not.
Taller boy: (voice getting deeper) Let's go.

The three assailants run off. Blake turns back towards the house.

Shock.

He didn't need to feel that. Danielle, Grant, and Rick's faces painted that emotion clearly.

Grant: How did you…

The world begins to spin and goes black.

CHAPTER 2

Blake awakens on the couch to a wet tongue licking his hand. He looks down to see the dog sitting on the floor next to the couch. Danielle and Grant are sitting in his living room with Rick and Jeff. Blake lifts his legs and hold his head in his hands. He can feel his heartbeat in his ears.

Grant: How you feeling?
Blake: Like a semi-truck slowly rolled its huge tires over my head.
Rick: Have you ever done that before?
Blake: No. Excuse me.

Blake runs into the bathroom and throws up into the toilet.

Grant: Looks like it took a lot out of you.
Rick: Anyone want to tell me what's going on?
Grant: Prior to the event that you saw, your son was part of a supernatural event. That's the reason you the

demonic pet in your living room. The event you saw... you know about as much as I do.
Rick: Who were the people in the street?
Grant: Looking into that.
Rick: Are we going to be safe here?
Grant: I'm assigning an agent to protect you.
Rick: Doesn't make me feel much better. My kid did your job for you.
Grant: Your son summoned a demonic pet and exhibited special abilities out of nowhere. Even though I do this every day, I was surprised.

Blake walks up and pets the dog.

Blake: He doesn't seem demonic to me.
Grant: He did bite you.
Blake: Then he saved me.
Grant: True.

Tunk! Tunk! Tunk! There is a knock at the door. Danielle pulls out her hammer and Grant pulls out his gun.

Grant: You expecting someone?
Rick: Not this late.

Grant walks up to the door. A young man in a black suit is on the other side.

Fear. This guy is timid.

Grant: Hi Mark. Where is she?

An elderly woman in a pink sweat suit steps out from

Chapter 2

behind Mark. She smiles.

Woman: Here I am.

She pushes her way inside and the smile leaves her face. The dog gets up and growls.

Anger.

Grant: What do you want Mama Nancy?
Mama: What color hair does his handler have?
Grant: Why does that matter?

Fury.

Mama: What color!?
Grant: It was red, but she's dead, so why does it matter?

Confusion, fear, and anger.

Mama Nancy leans up against the wall.

Mama: If she's dead, he should have returned home. How did she die?
Blake: He killed her.

Amusement.

Mama: Ha! That's cute boy, but the adults are talking.
Blake: I was there when it happened.
Mama: Wait what?
Blake: When she appeared I ran into her.
Mama: And he killed her?

Blake: Yes.
Mama: You are mistaken. They were of the Unbound Bloodline. It is not possible for this beast to defy its master.
Blake: It's cute how you have ears for decoration.
Mama: Unbound are not part of the normal rabble. They are taken from the group so they can kill those within it. It would be useless to have a pet that your enemy can control. The pets have a near unbreakable empathic bond with their handler and only listen to them. The Blood Queen herself cannot control an Unbound pet. That's why the handler's hair is red, to show their loyalty to the Blood Queen. This pet did not kill its master!
Blake: I know what I saw.
Mama: You are too stupid to understand.

The dog lunges at Mama Nancy. A sheet of ice stops its advance.

Fear.

Blake: Sit.

The dog walks back to Blake's side and sits.

Mama: (Shaking) He listens to you!

She sits on the ground.

Mama: A human BOY! This makes no sense.
Rick: Lady, why does this affect you?
Mama: Because that mutt was here to kill me!

Chapter 2

Anger.

Blake: Well he's not going to kill you if I'm controlling him.
Mama: He just went for my throat!
Blake: Well don't argue with me, and you will be fine.
Mama: Ha! You are a child, you cannot maintain the lifeforce needed to sustain this beast.
Mark: If I may intervene. This appears to be the boy that dispatched Shane and the other two.
Mama: Oh when you did nothing?
Mark: I assumed they were going to be slaughtered, I wasn't going to jump into that.
Mama: So useful.
Mark: This boy does not have ill intentions. You'll be fine.
Mama: Fine. Let's go.
Blake: Wait, what do I feed him?
Mama: Nothing, he feeds off of you through the empathic link. You will have to ensure you keep yourself in top health so he remains in top health too.
Blake: Seems simple enough.
Rick: Wait, this demon is going to feed off of my kid?
Mama: Yes.
Rick: And if I'm not ok with that?
Mama: I have no idea how he formed this link with the pet, but it is not breakable.
Rick: Can Blake die from this?
Mama: If he is a good handler, the beast will be loyal, and not take from Blake when it will hurt him. If the beast is too powerful, it will drain him until he dies.
Rick: That's just great.
Mama: I need a smoke and a beer. Let's go Mark.

Sadness.

Mark: Ok.

Mama Nancy and Mark open the door and leave.

Rick: She's a wonderful lady.
Grant: At least we know who came after Blake and why.
Rick: And that's a good thing?
Grant: She won't bother him as long as he doesn't bother her.
Rick: I'm more worried about the thing feeding off my son.
Grant: We will continue to keep an eye on Blake. I will also have the tech's look into a way to break the link she talked about.
Rick: That doesn't make me feel better.
Grant: Just doing what I can.

Blake gets a shiver in his spine, but he feels no emotion.

Blake: Pretty sure there is something on the outside of the door.

Grant walk up and opens it. A man of average height stands at the door. His brown hair is cut so short it's difficult to see. His black suit like it's about to burst.

Grant: Hi Scythe.
Scythe: Sup.
Grant: Alright, Scythe will protect you guys. I have a tower of paperwork to do.

Chapter 2

Grant walks up to Blake and holds out his hand. Blake grabs it and shakes it.

Grant: It was a pleasure to meet you. I'll see you again soon.
Blake: Thanks, it was nice to meet you guys too.

Danielle walks up and hugs Blake.

Surprise. Surprise.

Scythe looks at Grant with confusion.

Grant: Don't ask me man. She's been acting weird since we met Blake.

Grant and Danielle leave the room. Rick holds out his hand to Scythe.

Rick: I'm Rick. Nice to meet you.

Scythe bows.

Scythe: Nice to meet you, they call me Scythe.
Blake: Is that a codename?
Scythe: I just have really cool parents.
Rick: Alright, I'm hoping I wake up and this was all a dream.
Blake: Night dad.
Rick: Night Blake.

Scythe leans up against the wall and closes his eyes.

Blake: So what can you do?
Scythe: I'm kind of strong.
Blake: Oh alright. That why you don't shake hands?
Scythe: You're quicker than most.
Blake: I'm a quick read on people.
Scythe: Good skill to have.
Blake: Do you want to sleep on the couch?
Scythe: I'm good.
Blake: Ok, well let me know if you need anything.

Blake walks into his room. He is followed by the dog. Blake sits on his bed and the dog lays down next to it. Blake looks at the slashes on his side.

Blake: You need a name.

The dog looks up and tilts its head.

Blake: Hmmm... Slash? No. Gash? No. Definitely thinking a G name. Gash, Gouge, Gauge? What do you think of Gauge?

Joy.

Blake: Gauge it is. Time for bed. Please don't eat me or anything while I sleep.

Confusion.

Blake: You'll get my humor eventually.

Blake closes his eyes and the room goes dark. *Beep! Beep! Beep!* He jumps at the sound of his alarm. *Tik!*

Chapter 2

Gauge turns it off with his nose.

Blake: Thanks.

Blake gets up and throws on some different clothes.

Joy. Exhaustion. I wonder what everyone is up too.

Blake walks out to the garage. Rick and Jeff are working on a car.

Blake: Looks like you got that bolt off.
Jeff: Yeah, thanks to Scythe.
Scythe: Meh.
Blake: So do you have to walk me to school?
Scythe: Yep.
Blake: Are you going to class with me?
Scythe: No.

Scythe pulls out a watch. He tosses it to Blake.

Scythe: Put it on. It will allow me to find you if you get in trouble.

Blake puts on the watch and looks it over.

Blake: Push the red button?
Scythe: Simple enough?
Blake: Sure.
Rick: Have a good day at school Blake.
Blake: Thanks dad.

Rick walks up and hugs Blake.

Feelings of Power

Rick: Please, get into less trouble.
Blake: I like how you say "less".
Rick: You don't have it in you to get into no trouble at all.
Blake: (Smirks) True.

Blake and Scythe head toward school.

Blake: How long do you need to protect me?
Scythe: I don't know.
Blake: What are you protecting me from?
Scythe: I don't know.
Blake: Are they assuming I will be getting into more trouble.
Scythe: Pretty much.
Blake: How do they know it will be supernatural trouble?
Scythe: Because someone as powerful as you always attracts the supernatural trouble.
Blake: I'm powerful?
Scythe: How else do you explain beating three of Mama Nancy's goons?
Blake: That was fun.

They arrive in front of the school. Steve, Monique, and the tall guy are standing there waiting.

Anger. Anger. Anger.

Blake: (Smiles) What's up guys?
Monique: Where is my staff!?

Chapter 2

Blake leans back. Scythe pulls out the two halves of Monique's staff and hands them to her.

Surprise. Joy.

Monique: Thank you.
Blake: Can we call a truce?

Blake holds out his hand. Steve shakes it.

Steve: My name is Steve.
Blake: Nice to meet you Steve.
Tall guy: You going to tell us how you did it?
Blake: Maybe you guys can help me figure it out?

Monique walks off. The tall guy shakes Blake's hand.

Tall guy: My name is Shane.
Blake: Nice to meet you Shane.
Shane: So you have no clue?
Blake: Not really.

Shane laughs. He looks at Steve.

Shane: Instinct, that's how he beat us. We'll see you around Blake.

Shane and Steve walk away.

Scythe: That was easy enough.
Blake: I like them.
Scythe: (Smirks) They are an interesting group.
Blake: I'm off to class.

Feelings of Power

Blake heads into school and into History class with Mr. Mikla. Everyone sits down in their seats. There are four rows of seats in the room. Mr. Mikla is a tall man with short, black, and gelled hair. He has a smile on his face and stands at the front of the class next to the whiteboard.

Mr. Mikla: Welcome! Is everyone ready for class?

An overwhelming amount of apathy and annoyance.

Blake: I sure am!
Mr. Milka: Way to be Blake.
Student: You do realize he's only excited because it's Friday and he's going to give us a big assignment.
Mr. Mikla: You're wrong! I am actually excited because the museum has a new exhibit.

More Apathy.

Blake: What kind of exhibit?
Mr. Mikla: Rome.
Blake: Gladiators and lions? That's cool.
Mr. Mikla: Yes, and anyone looking for extra credit can go and do a small report on what they see.

Actually tempting. I'll have to talk to dad about letting me go.

The rest of the day goes off with little to no issue. Blake and Scythe are heading home.

Blake: Thinking about checking out the Roman exhibit in the Museum.

Chapter 2

Scythe: That sounds interesting.
Blake: So you'll come with?
Scythe: Sure will.
Blake: (Smiles) Thanks.
Scythe: You always this happy?
Blake: No, not even close. It has just been a nice last couple of days.
Scythe: Why do you say that?
Blake: I guess I just like crazy.
Scythe: Where is your dog at?
Blake: Gauge? I don't know. Hmm…

Blake stops walking and holds out his hands.

Blake: Oh great and powerful beast, aid your master!

The air ripples next to Blake and Gauge jumps out next to him.

Scythe: That was wicked.
Blake: I didn't expect that to work!
Scythe: How did he hear you?
Blake: Not going to question it.

Blake hugs Gauge and looks at his side. There are light-gray lines where the scratches were.

Blake: That healed up nicely.

They head home and walk inside the garage. Rick and Jeff are working on two different cars.

Blake: Hey dad, hey Jeff.

Feelings of Power

Rick: Hey Blake, how was school?
Blake: Pretty good actually. We got an extra credit project to go to the museum.
Rick: Extra credit, nice. When are you going to do that?
Blake: I was hoping I could go tonight.
Rick: You taking your bodyguard?
Blake: That was the plan.

Rick walks to a nearby workbench and pulls out an oil stained wallet.

Rick: Its donation based right?
Blake: Yeah.
Rick: Here's two fives. Put one in for going and a second if the exhibit is good.
Blake: Will do. Thanks dad.
Rick: Be home for supper.
Scythe: I will make sure he is.
Rick: You going to be eating with us?
Scythe: If you'll have me.
Rick: It's the least we can do.
Scythe: Thank you sir.

Blake and Scythe walk out and head towards the museum.

Blake: Alright Gauge, I need you to hide for now.

The air ripples and Gauge disappears.

Blake: Do you know where he goes?
Scythe: Not sure. There is talk that they can pass through dimensions, so it really could be anywhere.

Chapter 2

Blake: I'll have to ask Mama Nancy next time I see her.
Scythe: She lives right there.

Scythe points to a dilapidated home across the street from the museum. The street lamps around it aren't working and there is no visible light inside.

Scythe: Doesn't look like anyone's home.

Blake closes his eyes.

Exhilaration. Fear. Anger. Contentment. Joy. Sadness. Boredom. Hunger.

Blake: There's at least eight living things in there.
Scythe: How can you tell?
Blake: Getting eight different sources of feelings.
Scythe: That is amazing.
Blake: I've been able to do this for as long as I can remember.
Scythe: What about the kicking butt part?
Blake: That's new.
Scythe: Very neat ability you have.
Blake: She's really close to my house.
Scythe: Gauge was after her remember.
Blake: That's right. I'll have to check it out later.

They turn to look at the museum. There are twenty stone stairs leading to the entrance. Four large columns are the decoration in the front. Blake and Scythe walk up to the front door.

Joy.

Feelings of Power

A young woman is sitting in a booth built into the wall.

Woman: Welcome. The museum is only open for a few more hours.
Blake: That's fine.
Woman: There is a place for your donation. You are not obligated to donate, but we do appreciate it.
Scythe: Is there anyone else in there?
Woman: Just a few guards and another gentleman.
Scythe: Thank you.

Blake puts a five dollar bill into the donation slot. Scythe puts in a one hundred dollar bill. They walk inside.

Blake: A hundred bucks?
Scythe: It's just money.
Blake: Yeah, a lot of money.
Scythe: I guess.

They follow the arrows to the Roman exhibit. There are multiple mannequins with roman armor and helmets littering the area. Blake pulls out a notebook and begins to jot things down as he sees them. He walks up to a short-sword and attempts to draw it.

Scythe: Why don't you just take a picture?
Blake: I don't have a camera.

Scythe hands Blake a camera.

Blake: (Smiles) Thanks.

Chapter 2

Click! Click! Click! He takes pictures of the armor and the swords.

Scythe: A fan of the weaponry?
Blake: Yes. I've always wanted to learn how to fight with a sword.
Scythe: The basics are easy enough to learn. I could teach you if you like.
Blake: You know sword fighting?
Scythe: We are taught the basics of many combats to know how to defend against them.
Blake: Your agency is pretty thorough.
Scythe: When your policy is not to kill, your agents have to be more skilled at defending themselves.
Blake: You guys don't kill anyone?
Scythe: It happens, but very rarely. There are rumors of a division of S.T.A.T.E. that is just for assassinations. I'm not sure if they're true though.

Pain. Just a flicker though.

Blake looks around for the source of the pain. He walks over to the artifacts. There are necklaces and even what appears to be a crown in a display case. He catches a large urn out of the corner of his eye. *Click! Click!* He quickly takes pictures of the jewelry. He looks at the urn.

Pain. It's radiating from here.

Scythe: What's up?
Blake: This thing is radiating pain.

Scythe takes the camera from Blake's hand and takes a picture of the urn.

Scythe: You got enough info?
Blake: Yeah. I should be able to make a good report of it.
Scythe: Stand next to the armor and I'll get a picture with you in it.
Blake: (Laughs) Ok.

Scythe takes a picture of Blake and they begin to walk out.

Scythe: I'll get these developed for you tomorrow.
Blake: Thanks. I appreciate you coming here with me and helping out.
Scythe: You aren't in as much danger as we thought. I have to do something to keep busy.

Scythe and Blake chuckle then head towards home.

Scythe: So what's it like, feeling how everyone else feels?
Blake: It can be overwhelming at times, but I don't have to deal with it all the time. I usually just feel the strong emotions. I don't really know how to control it.

They arrive home and Jeff has food ready on the table.

Rick: Good timing.
Blake: Thanks. I got a lot of cool info.

They sit down and begin eating.

Chapter 2

Rick: Where's your dog at?
Blake: Gauge! Your Master needs you!

The air ripples next to Blake. Gauge appears and sits next to him.

Jeff: That's freaky and cool at the same time.
Rick: Do you have to be so dramatic about it?
Blake: I'm not really sure. It's just more fun for me to do it that way.

Blake pets Gauge on the head.

Rick: For a crazy demon thing, he sure behaves himself.
Jeff: That's not a nice thing to say about your son.

Rick and Scythe chuckle.

Rick: Shut up Jeff.

Jeff chuckles and they continue eating. After everyone is done, Blake clears the table and puts the dishes in the sink. Rick holds out his fist.

Rick: Ready.

Blake holds out his hand.

Blake: Ready.
Blake and Rick in unison: Rock, Paper, Scissors!

Rick holds out his fist as Blake covers it.

Blake: Sorry dad.
Rick: Yet another loss. I don't know why I don't just order you to do them.
Blake: Because you're a good dad that makes chores fun?
Rick: It's not fun when I'm the one doing them all.

Rick and Blake laugh.

Blake: Off to do my homework.
Rick: That's my boy.

Gauge follows Blake into his room and Blake boots up his computer. He pulls out his notebook and begins his report. Gauge lies down at Blake's feet. After an hour, Blake finishes his homework and lies down in his bed. Gauge crawls over and rests on the side of Blake's bed. The room slips into darkness.

INTENSE PAIN!

The feeling makes Blake jump up in his bed. Gauge jumps up growls. Blake scans the house.

It's not coming from inside the house.

He looks toward the museum.

It didn't feel like this when I was standing right next to it.

Blake runs out of his room. Scythe is standing against the living room wall with his arms crossed over his chest. His eyes are closed.

Chapter 2

Blake: Scythe?

Scythe's eyes slowly open.

Scythe: (Slightly groggy) What's up?
Blake: I'm feeling pain from the museum.
Scythe: I'll check it out.
Blake: How are you supposed to watch me from over there?
Scythe: You're pretty crafty. Do exactly as I say.
Blake: Yes sir.

Blake, Scythe, and Gauge run to the museum. It looks ominous in the moonlight. They walk up to the front door. Blake pulls a five dollar bill from his pocket and puts it into the donation slot.

Scythe: Really?
Blake: I forgot to put it in when we left.

Scythe sticks an odd looking gem on the door. He pushes on the door. *Tunk!* Something metal snaps. Blake, Scythe, and Gauge run to the Roman exhibit. Scythe signals Blake to hide.

Blake: Gauge, hide.

The air ripples and Gauge disappears. Scythe and Blake move stealthily. They see a man in a long burgundy coat. His brown hair is slicked back. Blake gets an uneasy feeling from him. The urn is broken on the ground. The ashes have been placed into a large mound in the middle of the floor. They are floating above the mound and turning into a skeleton. The ashes continue funneling in creating muscle and skin. They do this until a bald, tattooed man kneels before the man in the burgundy coat.

Joy. Pain.

Man: Now Scipio, try to remain calm.
Scipio: Where am I?
Man: You are quite far from Rome my friend.
Scipio: Who are you?
Man: I am Jonathon, a friend. I have heard your legend and your tragedy.
Scipio: How did you bring me back?
Jonathon: That is not important.

Rage.

BAM! Thud! Jonathon is thrown into the wall.

Scipio: I will decide what is important.

Scipio picks up one of the short-swords and walks up to Jonathon. *Ting!* He swings the sword and comes in contact with a knife. Scythe steps out.

Scythe: I can't have you two scrapping next to such valuable pieces of history.

Surprise. Anger.

Scipio blurs next to Scythe and swings his blade. Scythe grabs Scipio's sword arm and lifts him up.

Chapter 2

Scythe: That's not very nice.

Scipio kicks off Scythe's chest and lands about ten feet away. Scythe cracks his fingers.

Anticipation. Excitement.

Scipio blurs in again and swings the sword wildly. At least it appears to be wildly, the sword strikes are precise and barely miss Scythe each time. Scythe grabs Scipio's other arm and swings behind him. *Crack! Pop! BAM!*

Pain.

Scythe breaks Scipio's arm and pushes him into the ground.

Jonathon: You could've killed him.
Scythe: Not my policy to kill.
Scipio: A fool's choice.

Scipio kicks Scythe's legs out from under him. Scipio moves quickly and stands above Scythe. *BAM!* Scythe kicks Scipio in the chest and sends him reeling back. *Tchhhh!* Scipio's sword scrapes across the floor. *Crick-aCrack!* His arm returns to normal.

Scythe: Vampire?
Jonathon: Very astute observation sir.
Scythe: You going to knock it off or keep coming after me?
Scipio: I plan to remove your head from your shoulders.

Scythe throws off his suit jacket and picks up a brick from the display.

Scipio: You mean to take me on with a rock?

Dadoom! It happens so fast that Blake barely sees it. *TaTink!* Scipio's sword lands on the ground. The brick no longer resides in Scythe's hand. Scipio sits unconscious in the wall. He and the brick are well acquainted. Scythe rushes over and pulls Scipio out of the wall. He handcuffs his broken arms and attaches a restraint on his neck. *Chachink!* The handcuffs attach to the neck restraint.

Jonathon: That was impressive.
Scythe: You going to try to stop me from taking him.
Jonathon: Not in the slightest. He is safer with you.
Scythe: Why is that?
Jonathon: He is older than most of those on the council. They will not like that.

Jonathon disappears into the darkness. Blake runs over.

Blake: Can't say I've ever heard of a baseball pitch taking someone out.
Scythe: He was either going to make me kill him or try to kill me. I had to surprise him. Grab my jacket.

Scythe pulls something from his jacket.

Scythe: Scythe to base, I am going to need a few good Mops.
Blake: Mops?

Chapter 2

Scythe: Work term.
Blake: So what now?
Scythe: We get him taken care of and then... We work on making you into an agent.

CHAPTER 3

Blake is awakened by the smell of pancakes and bacon. He hops out of bed and almost steps on Gauge.

Blake: Sorry bud.

He runs out of his room and sits at the table.

Jeff: Someone is eager for breakfast.
Blake: I am a growing boy.
Rick: Want to set out the plates and forks?
Blake: Ok.
Scythe: I got it.
Rick: Thank you.

Scythe goes into the kitchen and pulls out plates.

Rick: I heard a bit of ruckus last night.
Blake: We ran to the museum.

Curiosity.

Chapter 3

Rick: Why?
Blake: I felt pain coming from there.

Worry.

Rick: Pain?
Blake: Yeah, and a lot of it. I had to be sure everything was ok.
Rick: What was it?
Blake: A vampire resurrecting some guy from the past.

Surprise and Fear.

Rick: Did he hurt you?
Blake: No, I hid. Scythe took care of the Scipio.

Anger.

Scythe sets plates on the table.

Rick: Why is my son going with you on your crazy business?
Scythe: You ever tried to tell him not to do something?

Anger.

Rick: I don't want him in danger.
Scythe: If he wasn't in danger, I wouldn't be here.
Rick: I can protect my son!

Scythe picks Rick up by the throat.

Scythe: And snap you're dead.

Scythe sets Rick back on the chair.

Sadness and worry.

Scythe: And I like you, anyone after Blake will more than likely, not.
Rick: So I have no say what happens to my son?
Scythe: On the contrary, you make the decisions on how he is going to make it in this crazy world.
Rick: I don't want him going on any crazy quests with you.
Scythe: What about training him to deal with these things?
Rick: Like what?
Scythe: S.T.A.T.E. has a Junior Agent program for promising people. Blake has my recommendation to get in.
Rick: Do you recommend just anyone?
Scythe: Blake is the first one I have ever recommended.

Pride.

Rick: Here's the deal. Only on weekends and maybe a few weekdays if your homework is done.

Blake jumps up out of his chair.

Blake: Yes! Thanks dad.
Rick: Now Scythe, I'm expecting you to hold him to the highest standard. I also want you to keep him out of as much danger as possible.
Scythe: Deal.

Chapter 3

Rick: And Blake, I'm expecting you to do your best. I also expect you to tell me if it's too much for you.
Blake: Yes sir.

Worry.

Rick: Now let's eat this food your Uncle Jeff prepared for us.

Jeff brings the food out and everyone digs in. Blake finishes his food and brings his plate into the kitchen. He snaps his fingers. Gauge appears in the kitchen. Blake sets the plate in front of him.

Confusion.

Blake: You can lick the plate if you want.

Confusion.

Blake: I guess you don't feel hungry. Let me know if you need anything.

Blake looks Gauge in the eyes. They look like pools of swirling blood.

That's cool.

Gauge walks over and lies down in the living room.

Rick: So he doesn't eat?
Blake: Or he ate wherever he comes from.
Jeff: I hope he doesn't eat babies.

Disgust. Disgust.

Rick: What is wrong with you?
Scythe: Yeah, thanks for that.
Jeff: He's a demonic dog, it's a possibility.

Rick whistles and Gauge walks over. Rick pets him.

Rick: You wouldn't eat babies now would you boy.

Joy. Joy.

Blake: He likes you.
Rick: I've always liked dogs and he is the best behaved one I've ever seen.
Blake: That's for sure.
Rick: Remember that little terrier we had.
Jeff: Yes…
Blake: That thing hated everyone! Especially Jeff.
Rick: Wasn't all that sad when he ran away.
Jeff: Hope he ended up on a nice farm somewhere.

Scythe and Rick snicker. Scythe finishes his food and brings it into the kitchen.

Scythe: Would you like me to do the dishes Rick?
Rick: No I got them. Blake looks like he is excited to get going.

Blake stops fidgeting.

Blake: What?

Chapter 3

Rick: You may be able to read people, but I can read you better than anyone.

Scythe bows.

Scythe: Thank you sir.
Rick: Do you need any money or anything?
Blake: I'm not sure. What do I need?
Scythe: We have everything you'll need.
Blake: Ok.

Blake hugs Rick and fist bumps Jeff. Scythe and Blake leave. Gauge is following close behind.

Blake: You better hide buddy.

Gauge disappears. Blake and Scythe walk up to a black sports car.

Blake: Nice.
Scythe: It gets me from A to B.

They jump in and drive off. After fifteen minutes of driving, they arrive at a large white brick building. The entrance to which, is covered with large glass windows. The building has the sign "STATE SECURITY" on it.

Blake: Security? That's funny.
Scythe: What else would you call us?
Blake: This isn't that far away.
Scythe: Yeah, we have multiple bases throughout the world. Mama Nancy didn't pick where she stays now.
Blake: She under S.T.A.T.E. protection?

Scythe: Under our watch.
Blake: Gotcha.
Scythe: Now before we go in. S.T.A.T.E. is here to keep the world in the dark about all this supernatural stuff. The less the people know, the more they can live their lives.
Blake: Understood.
Scythe: What you see here, stays here.
Blake: Can I tell my dad and Jeff?
Scythe: Just don't tell them the details.
Blake: Just the basics?
Scythe: Yes.
Blake: Deal.

They walk through the doors. A balding elderly man is sitting at a desk. He appears to be napping.

Scythe: Hey Harvey.

The man snaps up.

Harvey: Giddyup! Who's the kid?

Giddyup?

Scythe: He's the one that helped me catch Scipio.
Harvey: Oh wow. Come on in.

The air in front of them shimmers and Scythe walks forward.

Blake: A shield?
Scythe: Yep.

Chapter 3

Blake: Nice.

Scythe takes Blake into a room with blue padding covering the floor, walls, and ceiling. Danielle is standing in between three people. A toned boy is holding two sticks and staring her down. A young girl and boy are standing behind her holding up their fists.

Scythe: I'll be back.

Blake sits down and watches Danielle.

Intimidating and downright gorgeous.

The toned boy charges her. *Thud!* Her fist connects with his gut. She takes his weapons and kicks him into the wall. She whips a stick at the girl. The stick stops an inch in front of her face.

Girl: Ha! Got it! Oof...

Danielle punches her in the gut as well.

Boy: Why did you fall for that Payton!?

Danielle pushes her over and whips the other stick at the remaining boy. He dives out of the way. Danielle jumps up and lands with her fist an inch away from the boy's face.

Boy: It's not really fair when you take my weapons away.
Toned Boy: Like you could beat her with them anyway.

Danielle holds out her hand and helps the boy off the ground.

Boy: I'd last longer.
Payton: About ten seconds Cody?
Cody: Shut up Payton.
Danielle: Are you alright Riley?
Riley: Yeah, my pride is the only thing bruised.
Danielle: With as many times as I have beaten you, your pride must be in traction.
Riley: (Laughs) That's mean as hell.

Blake laughs and claps.

Anger. Surprise. Surprise. Joy.

Cody: And you are?
Danielle: Hi Blake!

Danielle runs over and hugs him.

Shock. Shock. Shock.

Blake: Hi. Are you guys training?
Danielle: It's more like exercise at this point.
Riley: Who is this guy?
Blake: My name is Blake, Scythe brought me here.
Riley: Scythe? Are they making you into a Junior Agent?
Blake: He said something about recommending me to do it.
Riley: That's all you need. There really isn't a "program". They just put you into situations that you can learn from.

Chapter 3

Blake: Sounds like fun.
Riley: (Smiles) It is.
Cody: What can you do?

Blake snaps his fingers and Gauge appears next to him.

Disgust. Surprise. Joy.

Blake: Cody was disgusted, Payton was surprised, and Riley was happy.
Cody: Why were you happy about that?
Riley: Shut it Cody. I've always liked dogs.
Cody: That's a demonic pet.
Payton: Still looks like a dog.
Riley: Yep.
Cody: So you're a handler and a face reader. That's not impressive.
Danielle: Fight me.
Blake: What?
Danielle: Let's show them what you can do.
Blake: I don't fight girls.
Danielle: Pretend I have a penis.

Disgust. Disgust. Amusement. Not an image I wanted in my head.

Blake's face shrivels with disgust.

Blake: No thanks.
Danielle: You knocked Monique on the ground.
Blake: I didn't know she was a girl.

Bam! Danielle backhands Blake and he falls on his butt.

Blake: You're not going to make me fight you.

Gauge walks over to Riley and lies down. With a shimmering light, Danielle's hammer appears in her hand.

Blake: Whoa whoa! I'm not going to fight you.
Cody: Then fight me and Riley.
Danielle: Blindfolded.

What is up with her!?

Blake: Fine.

Rip! Danielle takes off her sleeve and wraps it around Blake's head. Blake jumps up. Danielle escorts Blake to the middle of the room.

Confidence. Worry. Anticipation. Anticipation. Pretty sure the first two are Danielle and Payton.

Both the anticipations move to the wall.

Or not. Why are one of the guys worried about me?

Blake awaits his beating.

Cody: Begin!

Anger. Confidence turned to Anger and is coming at me fast.

Blake steps to the side and throws a punch.

Chapter 3

Pain.

His fist connects with Cody's face.

Amusement. Amusement. Amusement.

Riley begins laughing.

Riley: My turn.

Blake feels excitement coming at him. He quickly circles behind the pain.

Pain.

Cody: Ugh!
Riley: Sorry Cod, he was faster than I expected.

Blake shoves Cody with everything he has. *Thud!* Cody runs into Riley. They both fall to the ground. The sound of loud clapping fills the air.

Voice: That's enough.

Blake removes his blindfold. He walks over and holds his hand out to Riley and Cody. Riley grabs it with a smile on his face. Blake pulls him up.

Cody: I'm fine.

Cody puts his hand over his face. Blake looks to the wall and sees Grant standing next to Danielle and Payton.

Grant: Cody, go to the infirmary for some ice.
Danielle: Still think he reads faces Cody?

Anger.

Cody leaves the room. Grant holds his hand out to Blake.

Grant: Bravo.

Blake shakes his hand.

Blake: It was all instinct sir, I was almost peeing myself the whole time.
Payton: I can't believe you made Riley punch Cody in the face.
Riley: You're as quick as Danielle. By the time I committed to the punch, it was too late.

Danielle hugs Blake.

Danielle: Now it's our turn.

He squeezes her.

Blake: I really don't want to fight you.

She gets a pouty look on her face.

Danielle: Please.

Shock. Shock. Shock. I'm a sucker for that pretty face.

Chapter 3

Blake: Ok.

Blake and Danielle step to the middle of the room.

Excitement. At least you're excited about this. Who am I kidding, let's do this!

Blake takes a deep breath and the world around him slows. Danielle runs at him. *Thud!* He catches her incoming fist. *Thud!* He blocks her kick and jumps back. He's moving faster than he is used to.

Defense or Offense that is the question. What the...

The room blurs for a second. He shakes it off. He blocks three more punches and is pushed to the wall. He drops and kicks Danielle's legs out from under her. He jumps on top of her and restrains her hands. Grant hits the ground three times. Blake rolls off of her. He lies on his back breathing heavily. Danielle jumps on top of him.

Uh oh.

Danielle: And you were worried.

She kisses him on the forehead and jumps off of him.

Grant: Alright, training is done for today.
Blake: Just give me a sec.
Grant: Ok, yell lights out when you are ready to leave.

Rather not have to walk out of here hunched over.

Blake waits a few minutes.

Should be good now.

He jumps up and the room begins spinning.

What the...

The room goes black. He wakes up on a rubber bed.

Blake: What happened?
Scythe: They found you passed out in the gym.
Blake: That training must've taken more out of me then I thought.

A tall woman with short brunette hair walks up to Blake. Her nametag says Sara on it.

Sara: Says here in Lisa's report that you were bitten on the left shoulder by a demonic pet two days ago.
Blake: Yeah?

Sara points to his shoulder.

Sara: There is barely any hint that you even had an injury.
Blake: Ok?

Sara pulls out a folder and holds a picture of a torn up shoulder.

Sara: This is what it looked like when Lisa examined it.
Blake: Ok.

Chapter 3

She holds up a mirror. Blake is surprised by the result. There are tiny little black marks where Gauge's teeth sunk in, but they are the only evidence he was ever hurt.

Blake: What happened?

Slice! Sara cuts his forearm with a scalpel. Blake winces and holds the wound firmly.

What the! Why did she do that!?

Sara: I believe you have a regenerative power.

Drip! Drip! The blood falls to the floor. Sara pulls out a rag and removes Blake's hand from the wound. She wipes the blood away.

Sara: With my theory, the wound should be healed.

Blood continues to gush from the wound.

Sara: Or not.
Blake: Glad you didn't shoot me!
Sara: This doesn't make any sense. That bite should've taken a month or two minimum to heal.

Scythe grabs some gauze and wraps Blake's forearm.

Scythe: You find anything else out Sara.

She shakes her head.

Sara: Not on Blake. I investigated the pet.

Blake: Gauge.
Sara: Oh, Gauge. He had large lacerations on his side that have healed nicely. He appears to be in very good health.
Scythe: How is Blake's energy level?
Sara: The passing out could be a sign of the pet, Gauge, taking too much energy from Blake. I'm not seeing evidence of that though.
Scythe: So what is it then?
Sara: What is your ability?
Scythe: Overpowered empathy.
Sara: An empath? That's very rare. Empaths fall in the realm of psychics.
Blake: I can't predict the future.
Sara: Psychic is a generic term for a mental ability. Other examples of this are telekinesis and telepathy. How far can you feel things?
Blake: I don't know, like a couple blocks, not very far.

Shock and fear.

Sara: Are you saying blocks as in street blocks?
Blake: No, wooden blocks, of course I mean street blocks.

Worry.

Sara: When it was street blocks away, could you see the source of the feelings?
Blake: No, and one was in a stone building.

Confusion and worry.

Chapter 3

Sara: It is very possible that Blake's empathy is wearing him out. The few empaths that have been recorded could feel ten to fifteen feet away, and they had to see what they were feeling from. Have you ever felt overwhelmed?
Blake: Just when I'm in hospitals and stuff.
Sara: What is the most amount of people you have felt at one time without being overwhelmed?
Blake: Seven or eight?

Disbelief.

Sara: No really.
Blake: I felt a house full of people yesterday.
Scythe: Yeah he did.
Sara: And you had to sit down after.
Blake: No? We just walked into the museum.
Sara: How do you activate your power?
Blake: I don't it's always on.

Anger and disbelief.

Sara: How long have you been able to do this?
Blake: As long as I can remember.
Sara: So since you were very little?
Blake: Yes, I passed out in a grocery store when I was four because I could feel what everyone was feeling. Dad said I was special and had to avoid large crowds.
Sara: Then you went to private school?
Blake: No, we don't have a lot of money. Dad had me walk in and see if I was overwhelmed. I wasn't so I was allowed to go.
Sara: How are you even alive right now!?

Scythe: Why are you freaking out?
Sara: If everything this boy says is true, he is the most powerful empath ever recorded.
Blake: That's cool.
Sara: Cool? Try unbelievable. You need to see me every week at least once. You also need to see me every time you pass out.
Blake: You're a little demanding for someone who just cut me with a scalpel on a hunch.
Scythe: He'll be here.
Sara: I have tons of research to do.

Blake and Scythe walk out of the infirmary with Gauge close behind them.

Blake: So what's her deal?
Scythe: She cares a lot about the people and animals in her care.
Blake: She cut my arm open!
Scythe: We all make mistakes.

Amusement.

Blake: You're trying not to laugh right now.
Scythe: She just sliced you out of nowhere!

Scythe leans up against the wall and begins to laugh so hard he can barely breathe.

Blake: Glad you are having fun.

Payton and Danielle walk down the hallway.

Chapter 3

Worry.

Danielle: What happened to your arm?

Scythe barely catches his breath enough to speak.

Scythe: They needed to take a blood sample.

He resumes laughing.

Blake: Apparently Sara thought I had healing powers and sliced my arm.
Payton: Seems legit.
Danielle: Why did she think that?
Blake: My shoulder healed way faster than it should have.
Danielle: Weird.
Blake: Yeah, my arm didn't heal quickly.
Danielle: I'm sorry.

She hugs him and he squeezes her.

Scythe: (Wiping tears from his eyes) You ready to go?
Blake: Yeah I guess.

Danielle and Payton walk away.

Blake: Can I ask you something?
Scythe: I will not apologize for laughing.
Blake: I didn't expect you to. Why is everyone so surprised when Danielle is nice to me?
Scythe: Oh, good question.
Blake: Hide.

Gauge disappears. They hop in the car.

Scythe: That girl is one of the coldest people I know. She never smiles, laughs, or seems to enjoy anything. She hates to be touched and hugging her is death sentence.
Blake: I haven't seen that.
Scythe: You wouldn't. Whenever you're around she turns into a completely different person.
Blake: I wonder why?
Scythe: You're guess is as good as mine.

They arrive home and get out of the car.

Scythe: Back in time for supper.

Blake runs through the front door and snaps his fingers. Gauge appears in the entryway.

Rick: How was your first day?
Blake: It was actually pretty fun.
Rick: What's with the bandage?
Blake: They had to do some tests.
Rick: Everything check out?
Blake: Healthy as a horse.
Scythe: (Holding back laughter) Yep.
Rick: What about Gauge, they look at him?
Blake: Yeah. They said he seems very healthy and isn't taking too much energy from me.
Rick: Good news, make any friends?
Blake: Maybe, too soon to tell.
Scythe: Oh he's made a friend.
Rick: That cute girl that was here before.

Chapter 3

Scythe: Bingo.
Blake: Hate you both.
Jeff: She was a gorgeous! Do we need to have... the talk?
Blake: Dad and I have had the talk and it's not even like that.
Jeff: So if she wanted to get a little physical, you'd turn her down?

Blake feels his cheeks warm.

Blake: Going to the bathroom.
Jeff: I'll knock to make sure you aren't up to something.
Blake: Hate you.
Rick: (Smiles) Love you kiddo.
Blake: Love you too dad.

Blake heads into the bathroom and washes his hands. He scratches his arm. He twinges at the sudden pain.

Wish I had healing powers.

He heads back out.

Rick: So how do you like it?
Blake: It's still early, but I think it's going to be great.
Scythe: He is already impressing some of my peers.
Rick: Oh really? How'd you pull that off?
Blake: I got lucky.
Scythe: He took on two Junior Agents blindfolded.

Surprise and Pride. Joy and Pride.

Jeff: That's my boy!

Jeff throws up his hand for high five. Blake hangs his head and slaps his hand.

Rick: That is impressive.
Blake: It was all on reflex, I doubt I could do it again.
Scythe: You'll be able to take on ten people once we get you fully trained.
Rick: I like that you are keeping a level head Blake. You don't want to get cocky.
Blake: Oh I know. You taught me well Dad.

Rick hugs him.

Jeff: Let's eat.

Jeff brings out a tray of large baked potatoes.

Surprise.

Scythe: Did you wrap some infants in potato skins?
Jeff: They are pretty big huh.
Rick: You'll never go hungry at this house.
Scythe: I can see that.

They enjoy their supper. Blake slowly works his way to his room and lays on the bed holding his gut.

Should not have eaten the whole thing.

CHAPTER 4

Blake awakes from his food coma.

Hatred.

Blake feels warm breath on his face. He opens his eyes. Gauge stands above him.

Blake: (Groggy) What's up Gauge?

Anger.

Gauge bares his fangs and growls.

Blake: Knock it off, go hide.

Gauge jumps at him. Blake dodges and kicks his legs forward. Gauge falls off the bed. Blake notices the sheer amount of extra scars littering Gauge's body.

Crap. You aren't Gauge.

Blake snaps his fingers. Gauge appears in between Blake and the other dog.

Anger. Confusion.

Gauge tilts his head upon looking at the other dog.

Blake: You know this guy Gauge?

The other dog looks between Gauge and Blake multiple times.

Disappointment.

The other dog disappears.

Blake: Awesome, who was that?

Gauge sniffs the air where the dog disappeared. He lays down underneath it.

Blake: So we're just going to ignore this? Nice.

Blake lays his head back down.

I'll have to make sure I keep Gauge out at night. I don't want that guy sneaking up on me again.

Blake wakes up the next morning and hops in the shower. He slowly removes the bandage from his arm. The cut looks slightly better. This is mostly because it isn't bleeding.

Chapter 4

Blake: Wish I had healing powers.

He gets out of the shower and dries off. He opens the medicine cabinet. Due to the high amount of injuries Jeff sustains, the medicine cabinet is always kept well stocked. Blake grabs a roll of gauze and heads to his room. After getting dressed, he attempts to wrap his wound.

Rick: Need some help?
Blake: Yeah, thanks.

Rick grabs the gauze and wraps Blake's arm in seconds. The wrapping is so evenly spaced it's hard for Blake not to be impressed.

Blake: You are insanely good at that.
Rick: I get to practice a lot.
Blake: (Smirks) I suppose.
Jeff: Hey, it's been at least a couple days.

Rick points at Jeff's leg. Jeff places his hand on his knee.

Jeff: Oh yeah, forgot about that one. Today is a new day!
Rick: (Smiles) Yes it is.

Jeff and Rick walk out to the garage. Blake heads into the kitchen and heads to the cupboards. He pulls out a box of cereal and a bowl.

Scythe: How's it going?
Blake: Crazy night.
Scythe: What happened?

Blake: Nothing, just didn't sleep well.
Scythe: I gotcha.

Blake pulls the milk out of the fridge. He makes himself a bowl of cereal.

Scythe: You really seem out of it.
Blake: Yeah.
Scythe: You want to skip out today?
Blake: No, I just need to wake up.

That other dog was disappointed in Gauge, but why? I'm going to have a chat with Mama Nancy.

Blake finishes his cereal then gets up to get ready to go. Gauge walks up next to him.

Blake: Going to need you to hide bud.

Gauge disappears. Blake and Scythe head to the car and drive away. On the way to S.T.A.T.E. a beep comes in over the speakers.

Woman's voice: Hey Scythe.
Scythe: Hello Deputy Director, what do you need?
Deputy Director: You got the feeling kid with you?
Scythe: Yes Ma'am, bringing him in as we speak.
Deputy Director: I need to see him right away.
Scythe: You will see him as soon as we arrive.
Deputy Director: Good, drive safe.

The speakers beep again.

Chapter 4

Blake: Who is she?
Scythe: That was the woman that runs our base of operations here.
Blake: Why would she want to see me?
Scythe: Not sure. I assume she's heard of your ability and thinks it can be useful.
Blake: Is this normal?
Scythe: She wants results and does not care how she gets them.
Blake: She sounds... interesting.
Scythe: You'll be fine. She doesn't want to deal with the paperwork of you dying.
Blake: That's not very reassuring.

They arrive at S.T.A.T.E. A woman with long brown hair is standing in front of the main door with her arms crossed. Blake can see her blue eyes from the car. Scythe and Blake walk up to her. Scythe bows.

Scythe: This is Blake.
Deputy Director: Nice to meet you Blake. Second day as a Junior Agent and you already get a mission from me.
Blake: So yesterday counts?
Deputy Director: Sounds like you did some training, I'd say it counts.
Blake: Nice. Do I get a badge or something?
Deputy Director: The Junior Agent title is all you get for now. If you do well with this mission, you can call me Jane.
Blake: Sounds like a deal.

They follow Jane past Harvey and into a room full of people and TV screens.

Jane: Know how many Junior Agents have been in this room?
Blake: One and me.
Jane: Good guess. If you tell anyone what you've seen in here, I will neuter you myself.
Blake: Sounds fair.

Holy....

Jane: You will be assisting Pulse in investigating the death of a demon thug Kenneth.
Blake: Why can't I go with Scythe?
Jane: Because I need you to go with Pulse.
Blake: Understood.

Multiple pictures show up on a nearby screen. There appears to be men ripped in half and blood covering a large room. The picture shifts to a man with a bullet in his head sitting lifeless in a chair.

Jane: This is Ken. Feel around for what happened to him.
Blake: I'll do what I can.
Jane: Blood freak you out?
Blake: No.
Jane: How about gore?
Blake: No.
Jane: Good, because you are going to see a lot of it.
Blake: Shouldn't you have asked me this before you showed me the pictures?

Chapter 4

Amusement.

Jane: No. That was the test. You throw up on me or quiver when you answer my questions, then I know you're not ready.

A young woman walks into the room with a man in a suit. She has long dirty blonde hair with bright blonde highlights. She is holding a medallion in her hands and tossing it about. She is standing next to a tall man who has his arms crossed. His brown hair is a cut very short. What is visible of his hands are covered in scars.

Jane: Blake, this is Base and Pulse.
Blake: Nice to meet you.
Jane: Yay, how pleasant, get moving.

The girl walks up and touches Blake's arm. They appear outside of a brick building. Pulse shakes his head.

Pulse: Sorry about that.
Blake: She's hiding something.
Pulse: She's under a lot of stress.
Blake: I would hope.
Base: You ready?
Blake: As I'll ever be.

Pulse opens the door and they enter the bloody scene. The room is set up like a small concert hall. It is long with a stage at the very end of the room. Two bulging masses of muscle and blood greet them at the door. There are five to six other bodies torn apart and scattered across the room. Ken is sitting on the stage.

Blake: You didn't clean it up at all?
Base: My power won't be as effective if they do.

Base walks over and stands in the very middle of the room.

Blake: What can she do?
Pulse: Base is what we call a Crystal. It's a type of Psychic that can see a scene in her head to determine what happened. We have a few of them that work with us.
Blake: Why do you need me then?
Pulse: The Deputy Director thinks with a horrific scene like this you'll be able to feel something.
Blake: Other than sick, I doubt it, I usually only deal with living things.
Pulse: Just try, I'm not expecting a miracle, but the Deputy Director is.

Blake looks around at the bodies and walks over to Ken. Blood trails out of holes on both sides of his head.

Being this guy is the only one intact; I'll see what he's doing.

Blake walks over a few steps away from Base and takes a deep breath. He focuses on Ken.

Pain.

Boom! Boom! Boom! The blood in the room vanishes and the bodies turn back into people.

What the...?

Chapter 4

A man walks up to the front door and opens a piece of sliding metal.

Man: What do you... why hello miss, what do you need?
Woman's voice: I heard Ken was here.
Man's voice: She sounds like a beauty, let her in.

Blake looks over to see Ken sitting in his chair at a table. He has a large steak in front of him that he is stuffing his face with. The metal door creaks and the woman walks in. She has long brown hair and is wearing a vest with fur on it. The rest of her clothes are tight and show off her muscular body. Ken looks up from his plate.

Anger.

Ken: Rachel, how nice of you to visit. Kill her!

TATATATATATATA! Automatic weapon fire rips through the air. Rachel blurs and cuts down the five guards in a matter of moments.

Boredom.

Rachel: Apparently you know my name, but you do not know my reputation.

Tung! Rachel is grabbed and thrown against the metal door. She spits out some blood. Two huge horned-beasts stand between her and Ken.

Amusement.

Feelings of Power

She blurs and tears into the stomach of one of the beasts. The other beast attempts to grab her and is sliced across the face. As its guts are being torn into, the first beast tries to headbutt Rachel. She removes its requirement to do such a maneuver. The remaining beast charges Rachel and she effortlessly jumps over it. *Snap! Thud!* It falls to the ground motionless.

Fear and Anger.

Blake looks over at Ken. Rachel licks the blood from her nails, which are now two inch claws. *Crack! Crack! Crack! Ting! Ting! Ting!*

Ken fires three shots into Rachel. They hit the metal door behind her. She blurs next to him and throws the table out from in front of him.

Disgust. Pain.

She digs her claws into his gun arm and he drops the gun. *Snap!*

Pain!

She breaks his gun arm then blurs to the door. She opens it. A man in a black suit walks in. He has black slicked back hair and well-trimmed goatee.

Terror.

Ken: Ronaldo! What are you doing here?

Chapter 4

Ronaldo: Why are creatures from the Realm of Demons appearing?

Anger.

Ken: I don't know.

Intense Pain.

Ken screams.

Ronaldo: I very much dislike being lied to.

Ronaldo walks up to Ken and the room fades into the previously gory scene.

Blake: What happens next!

Base is on her knees and blood is flowing from her nose at a rapid pace. Pulse walks over and hands her a handkerchief.

Blake: Why is she bleeding?
Pulse: Her power is very taxing on her brain.
Blake: Oh I'm sorry.

Blake walks up and helps Base to stand.

Blake: We got all the info we need though right?

Anger.

Base: No! We don't know why Rachel slaughtered all these guys.

Surprise and Fear.

Pulse: Rachel?
Base: She's the one that tore everyone up.

Fear.

Pulse: That's horrible.
Blake: Who is Rachel?
Pulse: A very powerful werewolf and the daughter of the most powerful werewolf.
Blake: Explains the claws.

Surprise.

Base: Did you see what I saw?
Blake: Yeah, isn't that how it works?
Base: No.
Pulse: What did you see Blake?
Blake: Rachel came in here and killed everyone except for Ken. Then Ronaldo came in and asked Ken about the Realm of Demons.

Terror. Confusion.

Pulse: Ronaldo.
Base: How did you see more than I did?
Blake: Wait what? Pulse you don't see what she sees when she is using her ability?
Pulse: Never.

Chapter 4

Blake: Well then I don't know what happened.
Base: The only people who could see what I see are people like me or mind readers.
Blake: Apparently not.
Pulse: You're sure it was Ronaldo?
Blake: Positive. He walked in here and asked Ken about the Realm of Demons, and then Ken felt a pain unlike any I have ever felt.
Pulse: We need to go.
Base: Give me a minute.
Pulse: Grab a chair Blake.

Blake walks grabs a nearby chair. He notices it is covered in blood, so he grabs a cleaner one and brings it over. Pulse sets Base on the chair. He then runs over to the door and ensures it is locked.

Fear.

Blake: What are you afraid of?
Pulse: I'm not afraid.
Blake: Yeah, try lying to someone else.
Pulse: I'd just rather not be here if Ronaldo and Rachel come back.
Blake: There we go. I can understand that.
Base: So let me get this straight. You saw what I saw and felt what the people in the vision felt.
Blake: Yeah, that's what I do, I can feel what people are feeling.
Base: That is awesome!

Base stands up and quickly sits back down.

Base: What did Rachel feel?
Blake: She was bored.
Base: But she was smiling the whole time.
Blake: It was fake.
Base: Wow.

Blake walks up to Ken's body.

Blake: What can Ronaldo do?
Pulse: Why do you need to know?
Blake: I'm investigating.
Pulse: It is rumored he can make anyone feel anything he wants.
Blake: Horrible. Then I'm assuming Ken shot himself.
Pulse: What makes you think that?
Blake: If Ronaldo can do that. He put Ken in enough pain to kill himself to make it stop.
Pulse: And you know this because of the pain you felt?
Blake: Yes. I also know Rachel didn't do it because she wouldn't use a gun.
Pulse: Cause you and Rachel are friends?
Blake: She was disgusted when Ken used his gun on her. Plus look at her other victims, Ken's death is too clean.

Pulse holds out his fist. Blake is slightly taken back by the gesture. He bumps his fist with Pulse's.

Pulse: You are as impressive as Grant and Scythe said.
Base: Hey! Why aren't you bleeding?
Blake: I don't even know how I saw what you did. Don't ask me why I'm not bleeding.

Chapter 4

Pulse: Blake's mind is taxed everyday almost all day. I'm assuming it can take more stress than yours.

Irritation.

Base: I doubt that is the reason...

Creatures from the Realm of Demons. No way...

Blake: They're talking about Gauge!

Surprise and Confusion. Surprise and Confusion.

Blake: This happened recently, right?
Pulse: About six hours ago.
Blake: Gauge appeared three days ago, they have to be talking about him.
Pulse: It's possible, but why would Ronaldo care about Gauge?
Blake: Good point. Gauge is pretty wicked, but I just think that because he's mine.
Base: Well let's get going.

She grabs their arms and they appear in the room with the monitors. Blake catches Base as she falls.

Jane: Get her to the infirmary!

Two agents grabs Base and take her out of the room.

Jane: What did you find out?
Pulse: Rather not talk about it in here.

Feelings of Power

They walk for a few minutes then enter a very nice office. Jane walks behind her large desk.

Blake: Nice place.
Jane: Thanks. What happened!?
Pulse: Rachel and Ronaldo are the ones involved in Ken's death.

Intense fury.

Jane picks up a snow globe from her desk and crushes it in her hand. *Tinktatink!* Chunks of ice and glass hit the desk and fall off.

Jane: Is that all?
Pulse: I'm sorry Ma'am.
Jane: Jonathon resurrects Scipio. Rachel and Ronaldo kill a creep like Ken. What next? Andrew walks in here and slaughters all of us for fun?
Pulse: I'm sorry Ma'am.
Jane: Stuff your sorries in a sack! Did you find anything else out?
Pulse: They were asking about the Realm of Demons.
Jane: Oh so this is your fault.
Blake: Like I just opened up the portal to let Gauge in.
Jane: Maybe you were idiotic enough to find a book and read from it.
Pulse: We have lots of evidence to the contrary Deputy Director.

Irritation.

Jane: Apparently he can't tell that I'm messing with you.

Chapter 4

Blake: I figured it out right away.

Jane laughs and walks out from behind her desk.

Jane: You look a little shaken Blake, you alright?
Blake: Just kind of antsy.
Jane: Go train with the other Junior Agents before you head home. I plan on doing some training after today as well.
Blake: Yes Ma'am.
Jane: Pulse.
Pulse: Yes?
Jane: Make sure everyone is at their peak condition. I have no freaking clue what is happening, but we need to be ready.
Pulse: Understood.

Pulse escorts Blake out of the room and into a hallway near the gym.

Blake: There a bathroom nearby?

Pulse points to a nearby door. Blake walks in and is relieved that it is a one person bathroom. He locks the door. *Tshh!* Water runs in the sink when he turns it on. Blake looks at his shaking hands.

She killed all those people in a matter of seconds.

Blake looks in the mirror and his short dark hair looks darker compared to his very pale skin.

What have I gotten myself into?

He looks into his own green eyes. Tears begin to well up in the corners pf them.

NO! I can deal with this.

He shakes his head and turns off the water. He takes a few deep breaths and the color returns to his skin.

Exhilaration. That feels familiar.

Blake walks out and into a nearby room where Scythe is standing in a glowing circle on the ground. He is doing very slow pushups.

Blake: Looks like you got the memo from the Deputy Director.

Confusion.

Scythe reaches the top of his pushup.

Scythe: Weight circle off.

The circle stops glowing. Scythe walks up and grabs a towel. He wipes off the sweat drenching his head.

Blake: What is that thing?
Scythe: It's a magic gravity ring. It makes me weigh about five times more than I do normally.
Blake: Normal weights aren't good enough?
Scythe: Actually, they don't weigh enough.

Scythe takes off a vest he is wearing and it crashes on

Chapter 4

the ground. He removes two ankle and wrist weights that do the same.

Blake: Have I mentioned you're strong?
Scythe: Once or twice. Now what did you say about the Deputy Director?
Blake: She wants to make sure all the agents are at their peak.
Scythe: I'm always pushing past my peak.
Blake: (Laughs) Well then keep pushing I guess.
Scythe: Is this because of the mission you just completed?
Blake: Yeah, it was crazy...
Scythe: I don't need to hear the details. Are you alright?
Blake: Yes, had a weird experience today though.
Scythe: What happened?
Blake: Apparently I saw what Base was seeing when she used her power and I wasn't supposed to.
Scythe: So you used her power?
Blake: I guess, I have no idea how though.
Scythe: Something to keep an eye on. What did you think of Pulse?
Blake: He's a nice enough guy.
Scythe: I train with him a lot. I'm sure you will like him.
Blake: What can he do?
Scythe: Kinetic Magic.
Blake: Which is?
Scythe: He can form a huge ball of kinetic energy in his hands and throw it.
Blake: So he can literally throw a punch.

Amusement.

Scythe: (Smirks) Pretty much.

A warm embrace wraps around Blake's head and shoulders and his entire body tingles.

Scythe: Hey Danielle.
Danielle: Hi. I was starting to think I wouldn't get to see you today.
Blake: Me? They put me on a mission as soon as I got here.
Danielle: Oh really? How was that?
Blake: Other than the weirdness of the mission, the weird people I got to see and deal with, and being called the "feeling guy"?
Danielle: (Laughs) Yes.
Blake: Intense.
Danielle: This job can be that way sometimes.
Blake: Something I will have to get used to I guess.
Danielle: (Smiles) That you will.
Scythe: Oh Blake, Sara want to see you before you leave.
Blake: That's not going to happen.
Scythe: Either you go willingly or I carry you.
Danielle: I'll make sure he makes it.
Scythe: Thanks Danielle.

Blake follows Danielle out of the gym and walks to the infirmary. Sara is tending to Base when they arrive. Base is asleep in a hospital bed with fluids hooked up to her.

Sara: Ah Blake, Base has been telling me some interesting things about you.

Chapter 4

Blake: I just met her, there's not a lot she could know.
Sara: She believes your empathy could derive from telepathy.
Blake: Which is?
Sara: Mind reading.
Blake: I can't read people's thoughts.
Sara: She seems to believe you can.

Sara walks up and looks at the bandages.

Sara: You shouldn't be seeing a normal doctor for your injuries.
Blake: I didn't, my dad wrapped it for me.
Sara: Is he a doctor?
Blake: No he's a mechanic.

Disappointment.

Sara: He picked the wrong profession.
Blake: He has to patch up my uncle Jeff all the time.
Sara: Oh, lots of practice.
Blake: Yeah.

Sara begins cutting the bandages.

Sara: So how are you today Danielle?
Danielle: I'm fine.
Sara: That's good.

Annoyance.

Sara: Well, it's good to know you're a liar.
Blake: She's not lying.

Sara: No, but you are.
Blake: How?

Sara lifts up his arm to reveal there is no wound on Blake's arm.

Blake: That was an open wound this morning.
Sara: Well we will have to see if we can recreate the situation that caused it to heal.
Blake: You are not cutting me again.

Blake falls to the floor holding his head. Danielle clenches her fists.

Intense hatred.

Sara: I didn't even cut you.

Blake stands up with a blank look on his face.

Sara: Don't be a big baby. You know it's coming this time.

Blake tosses Sara to the side and she lands on her chair.

Voice: Security Breach. All available agents report to the Main Entrance. Security Breach. This is not a drill.

Blake and Danielle run to the front door. A large man is standing with the air rippling behind him. The muffled sound of a woman screaming fills Blake's ears and then abruptly stops. Blake jumps up and punches him square in the chest with enough force to break the

Chapter 4

window behind him. *Thunk!* It sounds like two rocks being slammed together.

Man: (Smirks) It's going to take a lot more than that to hurt me.

CHAPTER 5

Blake jumps up and punches him square in the chest with enough force to break the window behind him. *Thunk!* It sounds like two rocks being slammed together.

Man: (Smirks) It's going to take a lot more than that to hurt me.

Thunk! The man punches Blake in the face and it makes the same sounds it did when Blake punched the man.

Man: Well then.

Blake grabs the man's arm and pulls him into his knee. The man knocks Blake back a few feet. *DADOOM!* Scythe punches the man into the ground and jumps back to Blake. He wraps around him. *BABOOM!* Pulse jumps on top of the man and the air explodes around him. *Tshh!* All of the windows shatter. Pulse jumps back to Scythe. Jane and Grant step up and put the man into a giant iceberg.

Chapter 5

Jane: Is that who I think it is?
Grant: Yep.
Jane: What are the odds!?

The ice explodes and throws chunks outward. Grant and Jane make a huge ice circle that catches the stray ice. The man stands up and brushes himself off.

Man: That's not very nice.
Jane: What are you doing here Markus?
Markus: I'm here to kill every last one of you.
Scythe: Good luck.

Scythe jumps in and punches Markus in the gut. Markus isn't even fazed.

Scythe: Aren't we durable.
Markus: Unbreakable actually.

Boom! Blake punches Markus in the face and makes him step back a few steps.

Scythe: We'll see about that.

Blake and Scythe unleash a barrage of punches on Markus and he steps back a few more feet. Markus throws out both of his arms and throws Blake and Scythe back. A rippling bubble catches both of them and they land on their knees. The air around Pulse's hands ripples. *Voom! Voom!* Rippling orbs launch at Markus. They bounce off with little effect. *Thung!* Danielle's hammer crashes into Markus' skull. He swings at her and misses. *Thung!* Her hammer hits him square in the chest. He swings and misses again. She jumps back. *CARACK!* A lightning bolt is barely blocked by Markus' hand. Chains come up like snakes and wrap around Markus tightly. Riley and Cody stand in a hallway near the Main Entrance.

Markus: Any man would be overwhelmed by such a display of power, but I am no man.

Markus flexes and the chains shatter around him. Markus picks up a piece of the tile and concrete floor and whips it at Grant and Jane. Blake jumps in the way and breaks it in half.

Resounding surprise.

Jane: What's the plan boys? We can't freeze him or we'll give him more shrapnel to throw at us.

Blake runs up to Markus and unleashes more punches. Markus returns punches. Neither of them even flinches when they are hit. *BABOOOM!* Markus slams Blake into the ground and a ripple throws everyone back. *Thung!* Danielle hits Markus in the forehead with her hammer. He backhands her and she flies into the wall hard. She falls into a large pool of her own blood. Blake's face shows a mix of pain, hate, and fury. His skin turns as black as coal. Two black spikes erupt out of Blake's back and turn into wings. Red cracks scatter all across his skin. In movement that can barely be perceived, Blake knocks Markus into the ground and beats him without mercy. *BOOM! BOOM! BOOM!* Each punch can be felt by those around him. Blake takes a step back and falls

Chapter 5

backward. His skin returns to normal and he lies on the ground motionless.

The entire room fades into black.

Voice: Now why would you make a connection with that beast?
Blake: Where am I?
Voice: You should be dead, but I'm assuming you're just lying on the ground.
Blake: Why should I be dead?
Voice: That is an Archdemon you just hooked up to. Your body can't handle a connection like that.
Blake: Then how did it?
Voice: I have theories, but I'd rather not tell you.
Blake: Why not?
Voice: Because you'll be an idiot and try it again.
Blake: Good point. Now what do you mean connection?
Voice: You're power is a two-way street. You can see what others are feeling. Feelings are very powerful. They determine what wavelength your body communicates with the entire world. If you make yourself feel what someone else is feeling, you can synchronize your body with them and do what they do.
Blake: That makes a lot of sense. So I can do anything that someone else can do?
Voice: Now what would life be if someone gave you all the answers.
Blake: Who are you?
Voice: Yet another answer you will need to find on your own. There have not been enough truths revealed in your world for you to even begin to understand who I am.

Blake: Why are you talking to me now?
Voice: To give you a hint to keep you alive.
Blake: Which is?

Anger.

Voice: Do not make connections with demons!

A white ceiling begins to come into view. Soon white walls show themselves as well. Blake is in some sort of hospital room. A blonde girl is sitting in a chair next to his bed.

Blake: Hi?
Girl: Blake!?
Blake: Danielle? Since when are you blonde?
Danielle: Markus did a lot of damage to me.
Blake: So you had to dye your hair?
Danielle: No, it's my natural color. I have a regenerative ability that dissipates the color in my hair.
Blake: So you're ok then?
Danielle: Yes.
Blake: That's good, I kind of lost it when you got hit.

Embarrassment.

Danielle blushes.

Danielle: I heard. You actually knocked Markus out.
Blake: Yeah, I really hated him in that moment.
Danielle: Apparently you were quite scary.
Blake: I don't really know what happened.
Danielle: Neither does anyone else.

Chapter 5

Danielle holds up Blake's hand and he sees it is handcuffed to the bed.

Blake: No chance you're just being kinky huh?

Embarrassment. Why did I say that!?

Blake: Sorry.
Danielle: No, it was funny.
Blake: So... uh, are they going to keep me locked up?
Danielle: They said they need to make sure you aren't a danger to yourself or anyone else.
Blake: Makes sense.

They sit in silence for a bit.

Danielle: Did you feel hatred for Markus as soon as you felt his presence?
Blake: Yes, and it was intense too.
Danielle: I did too.
Blake: Is it because he is such a terrible person?
Danielle: Maybe, I just couldn't control myself from wanting to beat in his skull.
Blake: Yeah, I just kept hitting him until I couldn't anymore.
Danielle: Scythe said we looked like people on a mission.
Blake: I've never felt that way before.
Danielle: Me either.
Blake: You didn't hear a voice did you?
Danielle: No, why?
Blake: I heard one when I was passed out.
Danielle: What did it say?

Blake: It said that I form connections with people when I feel the way they do. These connections let me use their abilities.
Danielle: So you got your healing powers from me?
Blake: I'm assuming.
Danielle: That is amazing.
Blake: I really want to test it out.
Danielle: You just have to feel how the other person feels?
Blake: I believe so.

Danielle gets up and pulls a knife out of her skirt.

Danielle: Hold out your hand.
Blake: Don't cut it off.

Blake closes his eyes and feels the knife run down his palm. He shakes his head.

Blake: Ow.

Danielle cuts her own hand.

Pain.

He watches as the blood pools slightly in their hands. Danielle grabs a couple tissues and wipes the blood from her hand. There is no cut. She grabs a couple more and wipes Blake's hand. There is no wound.

Blake: You're amazing.

Embarrassment and arousal.

Chapter 5

Danielle leans her face close to Blake's. *Claclick!* The door opens and she jumps up.

Jane: Alright Feels, you gone crazy on me?
Blake: No ma'am.
Jane: Good. That was some impressive work.
Blake: What are you going to do with Markus?
Jane: With all the demon crap that has been happening the last couple of days, I had a collar brought here that was said to be able to hold an Archdemon at bay. Markus is wearing it in his cell as we speak.
Blake: Why was he here?
Jane: He said to kill all of us, and I assume that is why.
Blake: Why today?
Jane: Maybe he and Ken were friends and he wanted revenge. I have a hard time believing Markus has anyone he cares about, but who knows.
Blake: What about all the damage?
Jane: Grant and I cast an illusion spell over the door. Harvey's pissed because he has to sit on a different chair since his favorite one is broken.
Blake: Magic?
Jane: Yep, it's pretty useful.
Blake: Is everyone ok?
Jane: Thanks to you.
Blake: Probably couldn't do it again if I tried.
Jane: (Laughs) That's actually good news. We almost peed ourselves when you went full Demonskin.
Blake: Demonskin?
Jane: Markus' ability. It's why we kept hitting him with no effect. It's also the reason he is known as the Unbreakable.

Blake: Noted. I hope we don't run into too many more that can do that.
Jane: There are only two known people with that ability.
Blake: Markus and?
Jane: You.

Blake gets a shiver down his spine.

Jane: Whenever you are ready to go, you can.

Jane walks over and unlocks the handcuffs.

Blake: Thank you.
Jane: You're only scheduled to work on weekends?
Blake: Yeah, my dad doesn't want me to forget about my schoolwork.
Jane: Good man. I will see you Saturday.
Blake: You can bet on that.
Jane: Nope, I hate gambling.

Jane leaves the room. Scythe walks in.

Scythe: Sup killer.
Blake: Not much, she says I can go home.
Scythe: Good. You still going to need a bodyguard?
Blake: That's a big ten four.
Scythe: (Smiles) Glad to hear it. See you out here in five.
Blake: Yessir.

Blake looks at Danielle. He runs his hand through her short blonde hair.

Blake: I don't like the blonde.

Chapter 5

Danielle: It doesn't flatter me?
Blake: You'd look gorgeous with any hair color.

Embarrassment.

Danielle blushes.

Danielle: Then what don't you like?
Blake: You only have that hair color when you heal, which means you got injured. That won't happen around me again.

Joy.

Tears run down Danielle's face. She hugs him and holds him tightly.

Danielle: Don't make a promise you can't keep.

She kisses him on the forehead and runs out of the room. Tingling fills Blake's entire body and slowly fades. Blake holds his head in his hands.

She does have a point. I haven't even begun to understand what I can do and I'm making bold statements.

He lays back and snaps his fingers. Gauge appears next to him. Blake pets his head.

Blake: A rough night turned into a rough day Gauge.

Sympathy.

Blake: Thanks. There was a bright moment though.

Curiosity.

Blake: I almost kissed Danielle.

Excitement and Joy.

Gauge wags his tail.

Blake: I do not understand the connection I have with her, but she is so amazing. I've never had the urge to be so close to anyone like I do with her. You think it's just hormones?

Irritation.

Gauge puts his paw on Blake leg and stares at him.

Blake: Ok, it's not hormones.

Joy.

Gauge wags his tail again. Blake gets out of bed and shakes himself.

Blake: I feel great for just getting in a huge battle.

Confusion.

Blake: Nothing to worry about Gauge. I got it all taken care of.

Chapter 5

Relief.

Scythe walks into the room.

Scythe: You ready?
Blake: Yessir.

They head out to the car.

Scythe: He pees or scratches up my car, he's dead.
Blake: Understood.

Scythe opens up the backseat and Gauge jumps in. Gauge lays down.

Blake: Good boy.

They head home.

Blake: How are you feeling?
Scythe: My hands hurt a bit from punching Markus, but other than that, I'm good.
Blake: You and Pulse must wreck normal opponents.
Scythe: (Chuckles) I'd like to think so.
Blake: I think I'm going to like working with him.
Scythe: You better.
Blake: Who do you usually work with?
Scythe: No one.
Blake: Why not?

Sadness.

Scythe: I am skilled enough I don't need help.

Blake: What's the real reason?
Scythe: There are only two people I would want to work with. One works by killing and would never trust S.T.A.T.E. The other has no idea I work for S.T.A.T.E. and I'd like to keep it that way.
Blake: What if I become an Agent?

Amusement.

Scythe: Why do you think I recommended you?

Blake feels an overwhelming sense of joy and pride.

Blake: I need to tell you something.
Scythe: Shoot.
Blake: I was visited by another dog last night.

Anger.

Scythe: And you're just telling this now, why?
Blake: Because I have no clue what to think about it. It really freaks me out.
Scythe: At least you're alright. Have you seen it since?
Blake: No, but I don't think it and Gauge see eye to eye.
Scythe: I thought you could feel portals.
Blake: Not when Gauge or this dog do it.
Scythe: I don't know why there would be a difference. Did Gauge try to attack this dog?
Blake: He did protect me.
Scythe: Ok, make sure he's out at night, just as an extra defense.
Blake: Good idea.
Scythe: And Blake.

Chapter 5

Blake: What?
Scythe: Secrets don't make friends.
Blake: I won't hide anything else, I'm sorry.
Scythe: Apology accepted.
Blake: Oh! I heard a voice.

Confusion.

Scythe: When?
Blake: When I was passed out.
Scythe: What did it say?
Blake: That I can do what other people can if I feel the same way they do. Oh and if I try this with Markus again, I'll die.
Scythe: First one makes sense. Good to know on the second. Any clue who this voice is?
Blake: No. I want to say it was female, but that's kind of a shot in the dark.
Scythe: With your instincts, I'd trust that shot. Let me know if she talks to you again.

They arrive at home and head into the house.

Rick and Jeff: Surprise!

Blake jumps at the sudden noise.

Scythe: Wow, I didn't know it was your birthday.
Blake: I completely spaced it.
Rick: That's alright son, your dear old dad didn't.

A fast-food cardboard box sits in Blake's spot.

Feelings of Power

Blake: Is that what I think it is!?
Rick: (Smiles) You know it is.

Blake runs over and pulls chicken strips and fries out of the box. Rick sets a spoon and a jar of mayo next to Blake.

Blake: Best meal ever! I love you dad.

Blake puts a glob of mayo on his fries and begins eating. Scythe smiles and shakes his head.

Blake: (Full mouth) What?
Scythe: (Chuckles) Nothing. Happy Birthday Blake.
Blake: (Smiles) Thanks.
Scythe: So this is his only gift?
Rick: No, this is his celebratory meal.

Jeff sets a box on the table. Rick follows suit.

Blake: I have no clue what these could be.
Rick: You'll find out once you get done stuffing your face.
Blake: Ok.
Rick: So what kind of day did my boy have today?
Scythe: He saved the lives of about two-hundred people. That includes me.
Rick: How did he do that?
Scythe: Your son is a hell of a kid.

Pride.

Chapter 5

Rick: I don't need to know the details. He looks healthy as a horse.
Blake: How old is he today?
Rick: Sweet sixteen.
Blake: I'm not a girl...
Rick: Not what the doctor said when he delivered you.
Blake: Ha ha.

Blake finishes his food and sits still momentarily. He closes his eyes.

Never gets old.

Blake: Presents?
Rick: Go for it.

Blake opens his gift from Jeff. It is a handmade leather collar with metal spikes on it. A tag with "Gauge" etched in it hangs from the collar.

Blake: Nice! Thanks Uncle Jeff.
Jeff: Handier with more than just a wrench.
Blake: Come here Gauge.

Gauge walks over and lays his head on Blake's lap. *Snap!* Blake buttons the collar on.

Blake: Fits like a glove.
Jeff: Of course it does, I measured, twice even.
Blake: You like it bud?

Pride and Joy.

Blake: Oh he likes it.

Pride.

Jeff: Good.

Blake opens the other present, which is in a large box. He pulls out a thick heavy quilt.

Blake: Wow, thanks dad.
Rick: With winter coming, I knew you'd need some extra covering. You've always liked to be crushed under your blankets too.
Blake: Makes me feel all cozy and safe. Thanks guys.
Scythe: I'll have to pick you up something later.
Blake: You don't even have to. Just tell me what S.T.A.T.E. stands for?
Scythe: Special Tactics Against Terroristic Entities.
Blake: That's awesome…
Scythe: I'm still getting you a real gift.
Blake: Then that will just be a bonus.

Blake heads to his room and lays under his blankets and his new quilt. Rick, Jeff, and Scythe begin eating. Gauge lays down next to Blake's bed. The sound of a woman screaming fill his ears.

Panic, Fear, and Worry.

The sound of heavy breathing replaces the screaming. The heavy breathing stops and so do all the feelings. Blake wakes up covered in sweat. He holds his head in his hands.

Chapter 5

Worry.

Blake: Don't worry bud. It was just a nightmare.

Gauge whimpers. Blake pets his head.

Let's try this again.

Blake passes out. He awakes the next morning and gets ready for school. He presses his forehead to Gauge's.

Blake: Thanks for being here.

Joy.

Blake: Better hide.

Gauge disappears. Blake heads to school and the day is pretty uneventful until lunch. Blake is sitting at a round lunch table by himself. Multiple other round tables litter one half of the lunchroom. A tall, lanky boy walk up and sits at the table.

Anger.

Boy: You didn't happen to snitch me out did you?
Blake: No I did not William.
William: My name is Liam.
Blake: My bad.
William: I'll show you bad, I spent the weekend in a hold because of you.

William gets up and slips and falls.

Surprise and Embarrassment.

Blake: Maybe you should work on your balance before trying to beat me up.

William gets up and walks off. Monique, Shane and Steve sit down at the table. Shane reaches down and picks up a marble.

Blake: Nice work.
Shane: Meh.
Steve: Is it true Markus attacked S.T.A.T.E.?
Blake: Where did you hear that?
Steve: Mama felt the portal open up.
Blake: Maybe.
Shane: Mark said he felt someone reach above Markus' level of power, who was that?
Blake: No clue what you're talking about?

Amusement. Anger.

Monique: We already saw you take him out.
Blake: That sounds like a lie.
Steve: Mama would like to congratulate and thank you anyway.
Blake: Cool, does she do favors?
Steve: Depends what it is.
Blake: I need information.
Shane: Walk home with us after school, and you can talk to her.
Monique: I'm not walking with him.
Shane: Take the long way?
Monique: Funny.

Chapter 5

Monique walks off.

Blake: Not going to jump me are you?

Amusement. Amusement.

Shane: Already tried that.
Steve: Didn't work.

Blake nod and smiles.

Blake: Ok. You guys don't hold as much hate as Monique does.
Shane: I'm not the hateful type.
Steve: She is very much the hateful type.

The rest of the day is fairly uneventful. Blake meets Scythe outside.

Blake: I got an invite to Mama Nancy's house.
Scythe: Oh, looking for info?
Blake: Yeah. She also wanted to thank me for taking out Markus.
Scythe: How does she know that?
Blake: Apparently she had people watching.
Scythe: Oh I suppose. Markus came through a portal and she felt it.
Blake: I felt it too. It brought me to my knees.
Scythe: That sounds terrible.
Blake: Yeah, don't remember too much after that.

Shane and Steve walk up.

Feelings of Power

Blake: She really doesn't want to walk with us?
Steve: She's spiteful as hell.
Blake: Oh well.

They walk toward Mama Nancy's. Blake feels like they are being followed. He turns back to see Monique and a short girl with brown hair. The girl is being followed by a cat and a dog. She has a white mouse on her shoulder.

Blake: Who's the girl with Monique?

Steve glances back.

Steve: That's Taylor. She's walking with Monique out of guilt.
Blake: Guilt?
Steve: We're terrible traitors, blah blah blah.
Blake: Oh why wasn't she with you when you fought me?
Shane: She's not violent like us.
Blake: Oh alright.

They arrive at Mama Nancy's dilapidated house. Scythe stands on the porch.

Scythe: We'll see her out here.
Shane: Ok.
Blake: Don't want to get trapped?
Scythe: Don't want to have to punch my way out.

Blake laughs and sits on the steps. Mama Nancy steps out with her arms open wide.

Chapter 5

Mama: Oh Blake! So good to see you!

She hugs him and Blake feels uneasy.

Blake: Good to see you?
Mama: I sent my kids over to help you, make sure you let S.T.A.T.E. know.
Blake: I will.
Mama: Shane said you are looking for info?
Blake: Another dog visited me a few days ago.

Irritation.

Mama: I didn't feel it.
Blake: Neither did I.
Mama: Did you kill its handler?
Blake: No, I didn't see one.
Mama: Hmm...

She sits on a rusty chair and pulls out a black cigarette. She lights it and a thick black smoke oozes out of her nose. Everyone backs away from her.

Scythe: Is that a triple six?
Mama: Yeah, why?
Scythe: Are you smoking them in your house?
Mama: No, I don't want to kill my kids.
Scythe: Good.
Blake: Ok? So what are you thinking?
Mama: Where is your pet?

Blake snaps his fingers and Gauge appears next to him.

Feelings of Power

Surprise and Excitement.

Taylor: That's cool.
Blake: (Smiles) Thanks.
Mama: You are getting very skilled at calling him.
Blake: It's not all that hard.

Curiosity.

Taylor holds out her hand.

Confusion.

Gauge tilts his head at her.

Scythe: What are you trying to do?

Fear.

Taylor: Nothing.

She pulls her hand back quickly.

Mama: I told you that wouldn't work.
Taylor: I just wanted to try.
Scythe: What are we talking about?
Mama: Nothing.

Mama walks up to Gauge and looks at him.

Mama: He is very calm.
Blake: Isn't he supposed to be?
Mama: Not typically. It has been quite some time since

Chapter 5

I've dealt with these creatures. Give me some time and I will figure out what is up with the other dog.
Blake: Thank you.

Mama Nancy smiles a toothless grin.

Mama: Anything for you kiddo.

The smile fades from her face.

Mama: Mark! I need more beer!

Irritation.

Mark: Ugh... fine.

Scythe and Blake head home.

CHAPTER 6

Two days have passed with no word from Mama Nancy. Blake and Scythe are walking home from school.

Blake: Think she's blowing me off?
Scythe: More than likely, but it may be hard information to find.
Blake: True, I'll worry later.

They arrive at home. Pulse is waiting there for them.

Pulse: Got any homework?
Blake: Finished it at lunch, why?
Pulse: Want to go with me on a mission?
Blake: I sure do.
Scythe: (Smiles) At least he's excited.

Blake runs inside the garage and set his backpack on a chair.

Rick: Homework done?

Chapter 6

Blake: Yessir, completed it at lunch.
Rick: Be home for bed.
Blake: Will do.

Rick walks over and hugs Blake.

Rick: They said this was investigative, but be careful.
Blake: I will. Thanks dad.

Blake runs back outside.

Scythe: I'll keep your dad and Jeff safe.
Blake: (Smiles) Thanks.

Pulse signals and Base walks over.

Base: Well well Blakey poo, how are we today?
Blake: Umm… alright?
Base: You disappointed I'm not someone else?
Blake: Like?
Base: Oh you know.
Blake: Did you go back into my hospital room and use your power?

Surprise.

Base's eyes widen.

Base: What, no, why would I do that?
Pulse: Are you snooping on Blake?
Base: No, I would never.
Pulse: Mhm. Let's get going.

Base touches Blake and Pulse and they disappear. They reappear in a large mansion in front of a very ornate fireplace.

Pulse: This is a theft, so a lot less gore then last time.

Base stands next to the fireplace and closes her eyes. The room rewinds backwards until a shadowy figure appears next to the fireplace and moves backward to the wall. They begin to walk forward.

Pulse: What do you see Base?
Base: A guy covered completely in shadow.
Blake: And I'm not feeling anything from him.

The figure walks up and takes a metal box off the shelf.

Base: He's grabbing a metal box.

Anxiety, but not from the shadow.

Blake: I'm feeling anxiety from the box.
Base: What?
Blake: You heard me.

The shadow walks over to the window and jumps out.

Base: Then they leave.
Pulse: Ok, well they don't have the key to get the box open.
Base: What's in there?
Pulse: No clue, even the owner said they didn't know how to open it with the key.

Chapter 6

Blake: Where is the key?
Pulse: I have it.
Blake: So what's next?
Pulse: This happened yesterday. We are assuming the thief will be back to get the key.
Base: Who would break in the very next night?
Pulse: They like to do what no one would expect.

Anticipation and exhilaration.

Blake: Someone is above us.
Pulse: Get out Base.
Base: I can take a thief.

Anger.

Pulse glares at Base. She vanishes. Blake and Pulse head up the stairs. *Ting!* Two pieces of metal collide. They run up to find out what it is. A person in a black mask is locking their sword with the shadow who is holding a bladed tonfa.

Shadow: Not here to fight you man.

Bam! The person in the mask punches the shadow in the face.

Shadow: Really!? Really!? Let's do this.

The shadow pulls out anther bladed tonfa. *Ting! Ting! Ting!* They exchange multiple blows. *Voom! Voom!* Pulse throws a rippling orb at each of the assailants. The shadow flips and dodges theirs. The masked one cuts his in half. *Boom! Thump!* One half hits the wall, the other crashes into the shadow. The shadow crashes into a different wall. The masked one jumps over and lay's their hand on the shadow. The shadows dissipate from their body revealing a boy with long dark hair.

Anger.

Boy: Really!? How did you even do that?

The masked one is suddenly veiled in shadow.

Fury.

The boy tilts his head to the side and begins laughing in a high pitch.

Boy: Now I going to cut your head off.

BOOM! An explosion throws the boy and Pulse backward. *Thud!* The boy is thrown into a wall and falls on his face. Pulse jumps up and is punched in the chest by the new shadow. Blake moves in and is thrown back by a small orb of rippling air. *Tinktatink! Tsssss!* The metal box hits the floor and melts away.

Shy.

Pulse feels his jacket.

Pulse: No way.

Bzzt! The shadow disappears in a red flash.

Chapter 6

Blake: He stole the key?
Pulse: Yep.

Pulse walks over to the unconscious boy. He puts him in handcuffs and kicks his tonfas to Blake.

Pulse: Make sure he doesn't get those.
Blake: Ok.
Pulse: Couldn't use anything that guy was using?
Blake: No, I don't know why and that shadow made it so I couldn't feel anything off of them.
Pulse: Maybe you can't use magic.
Blake: Maybe, but I couldn't use what you were using either.
Pulse: That's magic.
Blake: Oh.
Pulse: It's alright, gotta figure out what you can do. Let's see if we can find out what these idiots were fighting over.

Base appears. She closes her eyes.

Surprise.

Base: Bleh, what did you guys do?
Pulse: What?
Base: I tried to replay your battle and I got nothing.
Pulse: Magical interference.
Base: I can see magic.
Pulse: Blake couldn't feel through that shadow, maybe you can't see through it either.
Base: Dumb!
Pulse: Let's go.

They reappear at S.T.A.T.E. Lisa walks up.

Lisa: I'll check him out.

Pulse, Blake, and Lisa walk into an interrogation room. Lisa bandages up the few wounds he has and Pulse places him into a chair and chains him to the chair. Lisa puts something under the boy's nose.

Disgust.

Boy: Ugh... what is that?
Pulse: Woke you up didn't it?
Boy: Smells like your mom.

Blake chuckles.

Pulse: Wow... just wow.
Boy: Why are you holding me?
Pulse: You stole something that didn't belong to you.
Boy: And what proof do you have it was me?
Pulse: Two of my fellow Agents watched you do it.
Boy: Just speculation, but pretty sure they saw a shadow steal whatever it was.

A young woman walks in and hands Pulse a manila folder. He opens it.

Pulse: Thomas. No known occupation. Multiple counts of stealing, trespassing, and breaking and entering.
Thomas: It's Tomi and that's all when I was a minor.
Pulse: Two weeks ago?

Chapter 6

Tomi: Had my birthday a week and a half ago.

Annoyance. Confidence.

Pulse: A known thief in a house that was broken into last night, and he's sporting a shadow outfit that was worn by the thief who took an item from the very same house last night.
Tomi: Speculation.
Pulse: Who were you fighting?

Anger.

Tomi: No clue.
Pulse: An old accomplice? A rival maybe?
Tomi: I work alone and a rival implies someone is good enough to challenge me.
Pulse: They took the item you stole and you are sitting here.

Anger.

Tomi: All I know is I don't have what you claim I stole. You can let me go at any time.
Pulse: I'm going to assume you took a blow to the head and that's why you can't remember anything. Sit here for a while and call when you remember.

Pulse walks out of the room. Blake sits down in front of Tomi.

Blake: What covered you in shadow?

Annoyance.

Tomi: A wand I got from a magic fairy.
Blake: You're pissed at that guy for stealing from you.
Tomi: Wouldn't you be!?
Blake: Isn't it in the thieves' code to not steal from another thief?
Tomi: I sure thought so. Restealing is not ok.
Blake: What was in the metal box?
Tomi: Alright, you seem cool, so I'll cooperate. It was a dragon testicle.

Blake laughs.

Tomi: Now go get me an adult so I can get out of here.
Blake: But we were having so much fun.
Tomi: As much fun as a cavity search.

Blake steps out of the room.

Pulse: He's a real gem.
Blake: He's just mad because he got out-thieved.
Pulse: Well he's right that we can't hold him for long. Jane is more worried about the fire sorcerer. I'm going to head back in to see if we can find what they stole.
Blake: What do you want me to do?
Pulse: It's getting late, you better get heading home.

Pulse opens the door.

Anger and Confusion.

Pulse: He's gone!

Chapter 6

Blake: How!?

Pulse runs his hand over his forehead. He closes the door and locks it.

Frustration.

Pulse: Base, bring Blake home. Blake, I'm sorry I brought you out today. Do not think this bad run of luck reflects on you.
Blake: Ok?
Pulse: Sorry.

Pulse walks off. Base walks up to Blake.

Base: Ready?
Blake: I guess.

She touches his arm and they appear by home.

Hatred.

Blake doesn't hesitate to tackle Base out of the way. They barely avoid getting bit by a demon dog. Blake snaps his fingers. Gauge appears and squares up with the other demon dog.

Fear.

Blake: You can teleport out of here if you want.
Base: I'm not leaving you!
Blake: Your choice.

Hatred and Anger.

Blake runs at the other dog and pulls his fist back. The dog jumps at him. Blake wraps his hand around the dog's snout and locks eyes with him.

Blake: I'm having a bad day.

Crack! He slams the beast's head into the asphalt. The dog gets up and wobbles. Scythe appears behind it and puts it into a choke hold. The dog's eyes soon roll into the back of its head.

Blake: Can you come with me to Mama Nancy's?
Scythe: Sure.
Base: Well that was horrifying.
Scythe: Hi Base.

Gauge walks up to the other dog and sniffs him.

Scythe: He's not dead, just knocked out.

Relief.

Blake: You do realize that he wants to kill me, right?

Gauge walks up to Blake and whimpers.

Blake: Yeah yeah, he's important to you.
Base: Where are you going?
Blake: To find out about this guy.
Base: Where is that?
Scythe: Mama Nancy's.

Chapter 6

Base: She a fugitive. You can't just walk over and talk to her.
Blake: Sure is windy tonight.
Scythe: Sure is.

Irritation.

Base: Fine, but I'm not going with.
Blake: Where?
Scythe: You're not making any sense Base.

Anger.

Base: I hate you guys.
Blake: Anger is different than hate.

Base lifts her hand in a rude gesture then vanishes.

Scythe and Blake laugh.

Blake: That made my day.
Scythe: Mine too.

Scythe picks up the other dog.

Blake: I was thinking of calling him Faker.
Scythe: Call him Faux.
Blake: Why?
Scythe: It's French for fake.
Blake: Fancy, ok, that's his name.

They arrive at Mama Nancy's. *Knock! Voom! Carash!* Blake knocks on the door and it flies off its hinges into the wall. The pieces fall to the floor. Shane, Steve, and Monique run into the entryway.

Scythe: You must be connected to me.
Blake: Oops.
Mama: I don't get back to you for a few days and you break my door down!

Mama peeks out from behind Shane.

Blake: It was accident.
Scythe: I'll have someone come over and fix it for you.
Mama: You better!
Blake: I have the other dog with me.
Mama: I see that, why did you bring it here?
Blake: So you can tell me who it is?
Mama: Odds of that are slim to none.

Mama creeps out from behind Shane.

Mama: Oh wow, it's your pet's twin.
Blake: Would explain why Gauge has feelings for him.
Mama: Shane and Steve, lock it up in the basement. I would assume you don't want it killed?
Blake: Not really.

Scythe follows Shane and Steve into the basement.

Monique: So you just bring your problems to us?
Blake: Who else knows about this besides Mama Nancy?
Monique: S.T.A.T.E. is a huge organization, they should be able to help you.

Chapter 6

Blake: True, but I'm not patient enough to wait.
Monique: Oh, so it's all about you.
Blake: Actually if you remember correctly, you attacked me first. Oh yeah and I totally forgot... These things were after Mama Nancy to begin with.

Anger.

Monique walks off.

Mama Nancy: Let's go to the living room.

They walk into a surprisingly clean room. Taylor is at a desk in the corner. It appears she is doing homework. Her dog is under her seat, her cat is on the desk, and her mouse on her shoulder. A crime drama is on the TV.

Scythe: Why didn't Mark come and greet us?
Mama: Because he's the laziest bodyguard ever. Mark! I could be dead now!
Mark: (From upstairs) Sorry.
Mama: Does he feel sorry?
Blake: Not that I could tell.
Mama: Twit...

She sits down on her couch and cracks a beer. The smell of gasoline fills the air.

Blake: What are you drinking?
Mama: Don't worry about it.

Scythe walks into the room.

Blake: Are twins typical in demon dogs?
Mama: No. They are quite rare. Even rarer in unbound pets. Impossible that both twins survive.
Blake: Why?
Mama: With twins, the evil and good tendencies aren't fifty fifty like they are in one pet. They are split amongst the two. Which means you have a good and an evil twin. What purpose is a good demonic pet?
Blake: None.
Mama: Exactly. They are usually killed as soon as this weakness is revealed.
Blake: So how is Gauge alive?
Mama: I would assume the handler enjoyed how easily he listened and liked having an expendable asset.

Taylor turns and notices Gauge. She gets up and runs over.

Taylor: Hi Gauge.

She hugs him then gets up and holds out her hand.

Mama: That isn't going to work.

Embarrassment.

Taylor: I just like to try.
Blake: What are you trying to do to him?
Taylor: I'm seeing if I can control him.
Scythe: You're a beast tamer?

Pride.

Chapter 6

Taylor: Sure am.
Mama: But Gauge doesn't have the connection to nature required for her power to work.

Taylor pets Gauge's head.

Taylor: I still like him.

She returns to her desk and continues working on her homework.

Scythe: So can you hold the evil twin?
Mama: Better than anyone. They also won't be able to track him here.
Scythe: Thanks.
Mama: I expect free beer as long as I am holding him.
Scythe: Done.
Mama: I should've asked for more.
Scythe: Yes you should've. Ready to go?
Blake: What is the Realm of Demons?
Mama: Where did you hear about that?
Blake: I overheard a conversation about it at S.T.A.T.E.
Mama: It is where your pet and Markus live.
Blake: Where is it?
Mama: Are you ready for that history lesson?
Blake: Yes.
Mama: When God came to Earth, it was a horrible place of war and hate. It was run by pagan gods and overrun with creatures other than humans. Even if humanity was going to survive, it would take them thousands of years to clear out all the rif raff. God had a plan. Send all the evil and hateful elsewhere. She created another dimension and Earth for the evil to live on.

Blake: Why not just wipe them out?
Mama: That's not very merciful. Anyway, that is when the great flood happened.
Blake: You mean Noah's Ark?
Mama: Bravo. The flood washed all the demons, Nephilim, dark creatures, and remaining pagan gods into the new realm.
Blake: How did the water know who to wash out?
Mama: Anything with a human or animal soul, besides the Nephilim, were saved and transported in the Ark.
Scythe: So it was much bigger than a normal boat.
Mama: Dimensional Magic is very helpful.
Blake: Why is it called the The Realm of Demons?
Mama: Demons are not the only residents of the realm, but they do own most of it.
Scythe: Where is the proof of this happening?
Mama: Just because you haven't seen evidence of something, doesn't mean it didn't happen.
Blake: Where are you from?
Mama: That is a story for another day.
Scythe: Are you the reason that the dogs are here?

Surprise and Anger.

Mama: Yes.

Mama Nancy stretches and yawns.

Mama: I think it's time for you to go.
Blake: Ok.

Scythe, Gauge, and Blake walk out the broken door.

Chapter 6

Scythe: I don't believe her on that last question.
Blake: Why else would they be here?
Scythe: I don't know, but she knows a lot more than she is letting on.
Blake: Oh that's for sure.
Voice: Why hello boys.

Blake and Scythe see a hooded man.

Scythe: Sup.
Man: I was following the trail of a dog very much like the one you have.
Blake: He's dead.

Anger.

Man: Then I will just have to add yours to my collection.

A portal opens up and three small demon dogs jump out. They are skin and bones and look very malnourished. They have different coloring than Gauge. Their bellies and chin are red. Their tails are also almost non-existent.

Man: Get them my pets.
Blake: Knock it off!

Fear. Fear. Fear. Fear and Anger.

The dogs stop their advance and cower by their handler.

Feelings of Power

Man: Your power is uncanny.

Gauge runs up and headbutts the front dog. It crumples like a pop can. The other two bite at Gauge. He stands tall and they cower. Blake runs forward and grabs the man by his robe. The man slips out and falls on the ground. He too looks malnourished. He is very thin and pale. He shakes with every move he makes.

Man: Aid me my pets!

Blake turns and looks at the three pets running at him.

Blake: Sit down!

The three pets sit.

Blake: Who are you and who do you work for?
Man: That is none of your concern.

The man pulls out a glass vial and raises it to his lips. *Fwap!* Blake grabs the man's arm.

Fear.

Blake: Nope.
Man: Get him my pets!

The dogs get up.

Blake: I said sit.

Chapter 6

The three dogs plant their bottoms on the ground.

Man: Kill him!

The dogs don't even move.

Blake: Who are you!?

CHAPTER 7

Blake: Who are you!?

Scythe walks up and takes the vial out of the man's hand.

Man: Kill them!

The dogs sit still.

Blake: Doesn't look like they want to listen to you.

Scythe grabs onto the man and Blake lets go. *Click! Click!* Scythe puts the man in handcuffs. *Thud!* Scythe pushes the man against a nearby wall.

Scythe: You got this?
Blake: Yeah.

Scythe pulls out his phone and dials.

Chapter 7

Man: My brothers and sisters will make you pay for this.
Blake: And where are they to make this happen?
Voice: Pierce! Is that you!?

Taylor runs up out of breath.

Disappointment.

Blake: What's up?
Taylor: Nothing.

Surprise.

She jumps at the sight of the three dogs sitting on the street.

Taylor: Those his?
Blake: He says they are, but they don't listen very well.
Man: They used to!
Blake: Who's Pierce?

Shock. Anger.

Taylor: Nobody.

She runs back to Mama Nancy's.

Blake: Why were you so shocked to hear that name?
Man: What name?
Blake: Who is Pierce?
Man: I do not know that name.
Blake: Then who are you?

Man: I won't be here long enough for you to have to know!

Blake looks around.

Blake: No one is coming here to help you.

Lights shine from the street.

Joy.

Grant: Sup Scythe.

Disappointment.

Scythe: This guy tried to attack us.

Danielle walks up and picks up the man's robe.

Danielle: Odd outfit.

Irritation.

Grant: Yeah it is. What's your name?
Man: You will get no information from me!
Danielle: Says on his ID his name is Mitch.

Surprise and Sadness.

Grant: Weird, you guys usually get punished for hanging on to stuff from your past.

Chapter 7

Fear.

Mitch: No, it's not that way anymore.
Blake: He's lying.
Mitch: Shut up!
Grant: What are we going to do with the dogs?
Blake: They're listening to me now, so what do you need them to do?
Grant: Load them up in the back of my truck.
Blake: Ok.
Grant: Tell them not to poop in there too.
Blake: (Smiles) Ok.

Danielle opens the back of the SUV.

Blake: Up.

The three dogs jump into the back of the truck. Blake pets them on their heads.

Danielle: They look so sick.
Blake: Yeah, I feel sorry for them.
Grant: Think you can take him in your car?
Scythe: Yeah. You think you'll be alright Blake?
Blake: I would hope so.
Danielle: I'll stay with him to make sure he's safe.
Grant: (Smiles) Ok.
Blake: You guys listen to Grant.

The dogs look at Grant and wag their tails.

Grant: Thanks.
Blake: Be careful, I don't know how long they'll listen.

Grant: If I have to crank up the AC, I will.

Scythe lifts up Mitch and puts him in the back of his car.

Grant and Scythe drive off. Danielle hugs him.

Danielle: How's it going?
Blake: Better now.
Danielle: What's up?
Blake: Apparently I can't copy magic.
Danielle: Eh, Magic is overrated anyway.
Blake: (Smiles) Thanks.
Danielle: You copied Markus' demonskin and my healing, why would you need magic?
Blake: Because I can't hang on to those abilities to fight on my own.
Danielle: Looks like you need to learn to fight on your own.
Blake: That's for sure.

Gauge walks up and bumps Blake with his head.

Danielle: Or use Gauge more.
Blake: I don't want him to get hurt.

Danielle kneels down and pets Gauge.

Danielle: He's pretty resilient.
Blake: That's true, but I'd still rather he not get hurt in the first place.
Danielle: I gotcha. Can we go inside?

Chapter 7

Blake: Oh yeah.

They step inside.

Rick: You're late.
Blake: I'm sorry.

Joy.

Rick: Hi, welcome back to our home.

Danielle bows.

Danielle: Thank you sir.
Rick: Food's still warm, Jeff we'll need a bowl for Blake's lady friend.
Jeff: 10-4.
Blake: I don't think Scythe will be back in time to eat.
Rick: Doesn't mean he loses out on his meal.
Blake: Oh I suppose.
Rick: What is your name again?
Danielle: My name is Danielle.
Rick: Well I hope you like soup Danielle.
Danielle: Soup is kind of a generic term.
Jeff: Just going to say Blake, if she doesn't like my soup, she's not the girl for you.

I'm going to beat you.

Danielle: (Smiles) Well I guess I better give it a chance.

Jeff sets a bowl in front of Danielle. He then brings out a large pot and pours a yellow liquid into her bowl.

Danielle: Some kind of cheese soup?
Jeff: Cheesy ham soup actually.

Danielle takes a big spoonful and eats it.

Danielle: Wow, and just the right amount of a smoked taste to it.

Pride.

Jeff: (Smiles) Glad you like it.

Jeff pours out the remainder of the bowls and takes one into the kitchen. He covers it in plastic wrap and puts it into the fridge. He sit back down and they begin to eat.

Rick: So how was the mission?
Blake: I wasn't too useful today.
Rick: Can't be useful all the time.
Blake: True, doesn't mean I can't try.
Rick: I taught you too well it would appear.
Danielle: You raised him very well sir.

Embarrassment.

Rick: Thank you. I've had a lot of help from Jeff though.
Danielle: I see, there is no woman in your life?
Rick: No. Jeff and I put a lot of hours into the shop to keep the lights on. It doesn't leave a lot of time for socializing.
Jeff: Not to mention always getting into trouble.
Blake: Hey, I've been good.

Chapter 7

Jeff: For a few days! And that's only because you're getting into a different kind of trouble.

Rick, Blake, and Jeff laugh.

Blake: I'll give you that.
Danielle: So what kind of trouble did you get into?
Blake: I like to hang out with the wrong crowd. The cops around here are big on "guilty by association".
Danielle: Well I'd say S.T.A.T.E. is a much better crowd.
Rick: They sure seem like it.
Jeff: Scythe has been a huge help around the house.
Blake: Yeah, he's kind of like the big brother I never had.
Jeff: I thought I was the big brother you never had?
Blake: You're the uncle I do have.

Jeff laughs.

Jeff: I'll take that.
Danielle: I hope I'm not crossing a line here, where is Blake's mother?

Sadness.

Rick: She died giving birth to Blake.
Danielle: I'm sorry to hear that.
Rick: It's not your fault for being curious.
Jeff: What about you Danielle? What do your parents think about you doing this stuff?
Danielle: I don't have any parents that I know of.

Shock. Surprise.

Jeff: How can you not have parents?
Danielle: S.T.A.T.E. found me as a baby. Grant said I was covered in vampire ashes, so they assumed vampires killed each other trying to figure out who was going to get to eat me.

Sadness. Anger.

Rick: I am so sorry.
Jeff: That is bull. Who eats babies!?
Danielle: Obviously they didn't eat me and S.T.A.T.E. has taken very good care of me.
Jeff: Well thank god they found you.
Rick: Agreed.

Blake holds up his soup bowl.

Blake: To parents! Be they single, adoptive, or just plain crazy!

Tink! They clink their soup bowls together and drink the remainders from their bowls.

Rick: Thank you my boy. Now don't think that gets you out of doing the dishes.
Blake: Of course not!
Rick and Blake: (In Unison) Rock, Paper, Scissors!

Joy.

Rick: Paper covers Rock!
Blake: Curses!

Chapter 7

Blake begins picking up bowls and taking them to the sink. *Tsshh!* He runs the hot water. Danielle walks over and leans up against the counter as he is scrubbing the first bowl. He looks over.

Blake: What's up?
Danielle: Sorry to hear about your mom.
Blake: Thanks, but I really never knew her.

Worry and Anticipation.

Blake: Someone is at the door.
Rick: I got it.

Rick opens the door.

Confusion, Anger, Hatred, Pain, and Anger.

Rick: Blake take a walk.
Blake: I'm not done with the…

Anger.

Blake dries off his hands and walks over to Rick. Rick hands Blake a cellphone.

Rick: I'll call you when you can come back.
Blake: Yessir.

Blake walks out the front door past a tan woman with short hair. He doesn't recognize her. She smiles at him as he walks past. Danielle and Gauge follow him.

Woman: Hi Blake. Since when are you a dog person Rick?
Blake: Hi?

Confusion.

Blake and Danielle start walking.

Danielle: Who was that?
Blake: No idea, but she didn't give dad good feelings.
Danielle: Want me to look her up?
Blake: No. If he wants to tell me who she is, he will.
Danielle: Where are we going?
Blake: Far enough away for me not to feel what's going on.
Danielle: That's quite the walk.
Blake: (Smirks) Yeah it is.
Danielle: This ever happen before?
Blake: Can't say it has. Gauge hide.

Gauge disappears. Blake grabs Danielle's hand.

Blake: Ready.
Danielle: (Smiles) Always.

They begin running very fast. They head to the park where Blake met Gauge. They sit in the grass. Blake lays back and closes his eyes.

Blake: Just not my day.

He feels warm weight on his lap and arms pin his wrists down. He opens his eyes to see Danielle on top of him.

Chapter 7

Her face is very close to his. She presses her forehead to his. His whole body warms up and he exhales.

Danielle: Better?
Blake: Very much so.

He feels the faintest graze on his lips and then she lays down next to him. She props her head on his shoulder and snuggles his side. He puts his arm around her back and brings the other arm in. It touches something very soft.

Embarrassment and Arousal. Oops.

Blake jumps up.

Blake: Sorry. I didn't mean to grab your boob.

Embarrassment.

Danielle blushes.

Danielle: Umm... you may want to sit down.

Blake looks down and instantly sits. He looks to the sky.

Blake: Puppies, flowers, chocolate chip cookies.

Danielle tackles him and presses her lips to his. He grabs the back of her head and rolls on top of her. His entire body feels like it's on fire. He grabs her butt, lifts her, and presses her up against a tree. She wraps her legs around him and squeezes him tightly. They kiss passionately for about thirty seconds and then press their foreheads together.

Blake and Danielle: (In Unison) Wow.

Beepdabeep! Blake sets her down and answers his phone.

Blake: Yeah?
Rick: Come, on back, sorry about that.
Blake: No problem at all dad.

Disappointment.

Danielle: Time to go back?
Blake: Yeah, when I can actually walk.
Danielle: Sorry.
Blake: You have absolutely nothing to feel sorry about.

Blake takes a few deep breaths.

Blake: Ok, it's not going away.

Embarrassment.

Blake: Well let's walk home and hope no one I know sees us.
Danielle: (Smiles) Ok.

He grabs her hand and they begin walking.

Danielle: Do you normally kiss the girls like that?
Blake: Never kissed a girl before, so no?

Chapter 7

Excitement.

Danielle: So that was your first kiss?
Blake: Yes.
Danielle: (Smiles) Mine too.

Fury and Pain.

Blake attempts to dodge but is thrown into a tree by a huge horned beast.

Voice: That takes care of him.

A figure steps out of the shadows. They are holding a chain connected to the beast. The beast is an eight foot tall Minotaur. Danielle's hammer appears in her hand. The Minotaur backhands her. She blocks and lands a few feet back. *Thud!* The Minotaur's eyes widen as it is struck in the gut. Blake delivered the blow. He takes a few steps back from the beast. His left arm is misshapen from crashing into the tree and blood drips from his mouth. *Pop! Crack! Pop!* His arm returns to normal.

Blake: (Spitting out blood) You alright?
Danielle: I should be asking you.
Blake: I am now.
Figure: Quite impressive, but you'll need more than a bit of healing.

A second Minotaur steps out.

Figure: Three on two.

Blake snaps his fingers. Gauge steps out. He growls at the figure.

Fear.

Blake: Three on three.

The second Minotaur walks up and stands next to the first. Danielle stands next to Blake.

Blake: We have these guys. Don't kill yours.

Gauge nods and disappears.

Figure: You're beast is a coward. Mine are bringers of death!

The Minotaurs charge. *Fwap! Fwap!* Danielle and Blake catch them by the horns. The bulls throw their arms forward. Danielle and Blake flip over them in unison. They land on their backs. Danielle jumps off of hers. *Clang!* She breaks the long chain holding it. The beast sits down. Blake's Minotaur grabs him and throws him to the side. It charges him before he can land. *Fwipwipwipwip! Thwap!* Danielle's hammer flies threw the air and Blake catches it. *Carunch!* It connects with the Minotaurs lower jaw. *Thud!* It falls to the ground.

Fear.

Gauge is behind the figure with his fangs bared.

Figure: Don't bite me little doggie.

Chapter 7

Anger.

Blake: Watch out!

Gauge jumps and dodges the figures lunge.

Figure: You think I control these beasts with my mind?

The figure throws off her robe to reveal a gaunt woman with short red hair. Her body expands outward and becomes much more muscular. She stands before Blake, Gauge, and Danielle.

Blake: So it's a girl.
Woman: You took my friend and now I will kill the both of you. Starting with the school girl!

The woman swings her massive hands ferociously. Danielle dodges them, but it takes considerable concentration to avoid getting hit. Blake charges at the woman. *Tung! Tung!* Danielle's hammer appears in her hand and she hits both of the woman's forearms. She almost connects with the woman's face, but the woman dodges and jumps back.

Blake: She's quick.
Danielle: Almost had her.

Pain and Anger.

The woman rubs her arms.

Woman: Ow! I'm going to crush the life out of you.

Blake: She's stronger than her bulls.
Danielle: Got a plan.
Blake: Actually just got one. You have her?
Danielle: (Smiles) You know it.

Danielle charges in and brings her hammer down on the woman. The woman blocks with her forearms. Blake runs over to the sitting Minotaur. He picks up the broken chain. The beast stands up and almost pulls Blake off of his feet.

Blake: No you don't.

Blake pulls with all his might and the beast quits pulling. *Carunch!*

Pain.

Blake looks over to see the woman's hand crushed under Danielle's hammer. She pulls it out and jumps back.

Woman: That hurt!

Blake moves the chain to the left. The bull moves to the left. The bull reacts the same when he moves it to the right.

Easy enough. Pain.

Blake looks over to see Danielle caught in the woman's giant hands.

Chapter 7

Woman: Got you now skinny mini!

Crack! Gauge headbutts the woman in the forehead.

Pain.

She rears back holding her face. Blake directs the bull at the woman and whips the chain. *Dumdadumdadum! Bam!* The Minotaur charges, slamming her into a tree. Blake jumps off the Minotaur's back and lands next to Danielle.

Blake: You alright?
Danielle: Yeah, she didn't even hurt me.
Blake: Sorry.
Danielle: Not your fault, she was quicker than I anticipated.
Woman: Show isn't over yet little punks.

The woman gets up and throws the Minotaur off of her. Her left shoulder has a big gash in it from the Minotaur's horn. Danielle and Blake blur right in front of her. *BAM!* They punch her in the gut together. Her eyes roll into the back of her head and she falls to the ground.

Blake: See we are a hell of a team, why can't we be teamed up all the time?

Warm lips press against his. He wraps his arms around her.

Danielle: Because it wouldn't be fair to the bad guys.

Blake smiles. Danielle calls S.T.A.T.E. Pulse and Base appear.

Pulse: She's tough on the eyes.
Base: Two in one day?
Blake: She wanted revenge for the first one.
Pulse: Makes sense.

Pulse walks over and picks up the, now very skinny, girl. He puts handcuffs on her and tosses her next to the bull. Pulse pulls out his phone.

Pulse: We're going to need a big truck to haul the two Minotaurs.

Pulse puts his phone away.

Pulse: Shouldn't take them too long to get here.

Pulse walks up to the conscious Minotaur.

Pulse: So demon dogs and Minotaurs?
Blake: What about them?
Pulse: This thing is calm as a cucumber. Are you controlling it?
Blake: Kind of. They are controlled by this chain.

Blake pulls it to the left side. The bull moves to the left.

Pulse: Weird. Can you give it commands?
Blake: I don't know. Sit.

The bull remains standing. Blake pulls on the chain.

Chapter 7

Blake: Sit!

The bull sits.

Pulse: Nice work.
Blake: I guess it's kind of a strength test.
Pulse: Isn't much of a test if you can pass it.
Blake: Ouch. I'm connected with Danielle.
Pulse: Oh, now it makes sense.

Tsss! Cracrink! A large truck stops on the street. Pulse picks up the girl.

Pulse: Any way you can have him drag his buddy?
Blake: I can try.

Blake pulls on the chain.

Blake: Pick him up.

The bull walks up and lifts up its partner. Blake directs the bull to walk into the truck's trailer. Pulse tossed the girl in the truck. Blake hands Pulse the chain. *Thud!* The bull drops its partner. It runs towards the front of the trailer. Pulse grasps the chain with both hands and the bull stops abruptly.

Blake: Impressive.
Pulse: Scythe isn't the only strong one.
Blake: I see that.
Pulse: Danielle, can you sit in the front with Base in case that chick wakes up.

Sadness.

Danielle: Someone needs to protect Blake.
Pulse: Scythe is at the house. Blake, you can use Danielle's speed to run there, right?
Blake: As long as it lasts I can.
Pulse: See he'll be fine.

Irritation.

Danielle: Yes sir.

She walks up and hugs him.

Danielle: I'll see you soon ok?
Blake: (Smiles) Definitely.

Joy.

She runs and jumps into the truck. Blake runs home at an increased rate. Gauge is right next to him the whole time.

Intense fury.

He looks up to see Jeff and Scythe sitting on the steps. *BANG! BANG! BANG!*. There is a loud metallic beating coming from the garage. Blake walks up to Scythe and Jeff.

Blake: Thought that was you.
Jeff: Not this time.
Blake: Better hide bud.

Chapter 7

Gauge disappears. Blake walks past Jeff and Scythe and heads into the garage. Rick is hitting a large piece of metal with a hammer. There are multiple holes in it. Rick stops when he notices Blake standing there. *Tink-tatink!* He drops the hammer. Blake holds out the cell phone. Rick walks up and grabs it.

Rick: I suppose you want to know who that was.
Blake: Only because I've never seen you act like Uncle Jeff before.

Fear and Sadness.

Rick: I'm not ready to tell you kiddo.

Tears roll down Rick's cheeks. Rick walks up and hugs Blake.

Blake: It's alright dad, just tell me when you're ready.

Blake squeezes his dad then walks inside to his room. He lays down. He snaps his fingers and Gauge appears next to him. Gauge lays down.

Never felt dad that sad or angry before.

He closes his eyes and the room goes dark.

CHAPTER 8

Voice: We'll see if that which you are so proud of, can keep you alive.

Fear followed by Excruciating Pain.

Blake opens his eyes and all he sees is fire and molten rock around him. He shakes awake and is covered in sweat. He breathes deeply and looks around. Gauge is looking at him curiously.

Blake: A terrible dream that I have no idea about.

Worry.

Blake: I'm ok. It wasn't real.

Blake goes into the shower and gets ready for school. Scythe is sitting at the table reading a piece of paper. A manila folder is sitting on the table.

Chapter 8

Blake: What's that?
Scythe: The report on your fights last night.
Blake: What's in them?
Scythe: Both of the suspects are members of the Extinguishers of Light.
Blake: Sounds like a cult.
Scythe: Not far off. They are a band of demon worshipers.
Blake: Fun.
Scythe: So very fun.
Blake: Why are they here?
Scythe: Mitch was trying to add Faux to his collection.
Blake: He could barely keep the three he had alive.
Scythe: Thane said it would be impossible for Mitch to have any more demon dogs without instantly killing himself.
Blake: Thane?
Scythe: One of our BioTechs.
Blake: Ok?
Scythe: One of our researchers.
Blake: Ok. Was that the only reason they were here?
Scythe: Probably not, but we're working on that.
Blake: Alright.

Blake heads into the garage. Rick and Jeff are working on a small black hatchback.

Blake: Dad, can I go to S.T.A.T.E. after school?
Rick: Sure, as long as your homework is done.
Blake: Deal.
Jeff: We are not going to be able to put a V8 in this thing.
Rick: That's what I told him.
Jeff: He paid half up front?

Rick: Yeah, but I think we're going to have to refund it to him.
Jeff: Nope. We're putting a V6 in here.

Jeff walks over to an oil covered computer on the side of the shop.

Rick: That won't fit in here.
Jeff: V8 is impossible, V6 is slightly possible, and that's all we need.

Amusement and Curiosity.

Rick: It's hard to say no when you are so confident.
Blake: (Smiles) Good luck.
Rick: Thanks, be safe.
Blake: I will.

Blake heads back in the house.

Blake: Think we can head to S.T.A.T.E. after school?
Scythe: I don't see why not.
Blake: Cool.
Scythe: Any specific reason.

I want to see Danielle.

Blake: Not really. I'm kind of antsy and want to feel productive.
Scythe: You caught two EoL people in one night.
Blake: True.

Chapter 8

Scythe laughs.

Scythe: It's not all adrenaline and fun.
Blake: Yeah, figured that out when Pulse and I dealt with those thieves.
Scythe: When you figured out you can't do magic?
Blake: Yep.
Scythe: Magic is for the weak.

Blake laughs.

Blake: Not really fair considering you can punch through a brick wall.

A flicker of Pride.

Scythe: Well what can I say to that?

Scythe and Blake head to the car. Blake stops and runs back in.

Blake: Better hide bud.

Blake hears a slight wooshing sound as he walks into his room. Gauge is gone.

Blake: Good boy.

Blake runs back out to the car.
Scythe: Had to put Gauge away?
Blake: Yep. I don't want him to be bored while I'm gone.
Scythe: Makes sense.

Feelings of Power

They drive to school. Nothing of note really happens except Mama Nancy's crew is missing. Blake meets Scythe at the end of the day.

Scythe: How was school?
Blake: Boring. Shane and the guys weren't there.

Worry.

Scythe: Let's check it out before we go to S.T.A.T.E.
Blake: Ok.

They arrive and walk up to the door. Scythe knocks.

Blake: How do you do that without breaking it down?
Scythe: Restraint.
Blake: You have a lot of that.
Scythe: (Smirks) Part of the job.

Irritation.

Mama Nancy opens the door. She looks very groggy.

Mama: What do you want?
Scythe: Blake says he didn't see any of your kids at school today.
Mama: So?
Scythe: Are they ok?
Mama: Probably.
Blake: Don't you care?
Mama: They all get good grades and are generally good people. I have no reason to worry.

Chapter 8

Scythe: Let me know if they are in trouble.

Irritation.

Mama: I don't have a phone or a car, how am I supposed to do that?

Mark walks down the stairs.

Worry.

Mark: What's wrong?
Scythe: None of your roommates showed up to school today.
Mark: They are off training. They told Mama Nancy before they left. They even asked for permission.
Mama: Oh yeah.

Irritation.

Scythe: Thank you Mark.
Blake: How is Faux?
Mama: Who?
Blake: The dog locked up in your basement.
Mama: Why do you insist on naming them?
Blake: Why wouldn't I?
Mama: For one, it wants to kill you, and for two, they are tools. Does a carpenter name a hammer? Does a mechanic name a wrench?
Blake: My uncle named his wrench.
Mama: Ugh... are you done?
Scythe: Is the dog alright?

Feelings of Power

Mama: Yes, he is sitting down there growling at anything that moves.
Scythe: We'll let you be. Thanks again Mark.

Mama slams the door.

Scythe: Must've woke her up from her nap.
Blake: I'd say so.

They head to S.T.A.T.E. and arrive to a fixed entrance.

Blake: Looks fixed.
Scythe: It is. Lots of overtime, but they did a great job.
Blake: Nice.

They head in and Harvey disables the barrier.

Harvey: Giddyup and Junior, how are things today?
Blake: Junior?
Scythe: He picks names at random as far as I've seen. Things are going good Harvey, how are you?
Harvey: This chair is hard as a rock. I miss my old one.
Scythe: I could break it in for you.
Harvey: Yeah right!

Blake and Scythe laugh and walk past the desk.

Scythe: I have training with Pulse, want to join me?
Blake: Do you know where Grant is?
Scythe: He's on a mission, why do you want to know?
Blake: I wanted to see if I could copy Ice Magic.
Scythe: You can try to copy Pulse's Kinetic Magic.

Chapter 8

I'm trying to find Danielle without asking for her. Quit having other solutions to my problem Scythe!

Blake holds back a smirk.

Blake: You seen his hands? I'm not having that happen to me.

Surprise.

Scythe: How did you know what happened to his hands?
Blake: Just a guess. He hasn't told me.
Scythe: I'll let him tell you. You could talk to the Deputy Director.
Blake: Oh ok.

Blake heads to Jane's office. Before he knocks on the door, he feels sadness.

Ok?

He knocks.

Jane: Who is it?
Blake: It's Blake, can I come in?
Jane: Come on in.

Blake steps in. Jane is sitting at her desk putting papers into a manila folder.

Blake: Something sad in that folder?
Jane: Did you feel me before you came in here?

Blake: Yes.
Jane: Knock it off.
Blake: I can't.
Jane: Yes, there is something sad in this folder, but I'm not going to talk about it.
Blake: Ok. Sorry.
Jane: What brings you here?

I suppose I have to continue with the lie.

Blake: I wanted to see if I could copy your Ice Magic.
Jane: I'm not a test subject.
Blake: Ok, just figured I'd ask.
Jane: Trying to do magic?
Blake: Yes. I'm not a fan of not being able to do something to help.
Jane: Well I can help with that. Follow me.

Blake follows Jane into a training room. A young man with piercings on his lips is punching a speed bag. He over six feet tall and his green Mohawk matches the green gauges in his ears.

Jane: Blake meet Adam.

Adam turns and holds out his hand. Blake shakes it.

Adam: Nice to meet you.
Blake: Nice to meet you.
Jane: Lovely. Now Adam, Blake needs the basics.
Adam: Yes ma'm.
Jane: I'll leave you to it.

Chapter 8

Adam throws Blake a pair of padded gloves and head gear.

Adam: Put these on.

Adam puts on similar gear.

Blake: What's all this for?
Adam: The basics.

Blake puts on the gear and barely dodges Adam's fist.

Blake: So no one two three go?

Adam swings his leg forward and Blake blocks it with both forearms.

Adam: I need to figure out what skill level you are at to determine what you need to learn. Feel free to hit back.

Adam unleashes multiple punches that Blake dodges.

I'm not feeling anything from him.

Adam brings up a knee that Blake blocks. *Bam!* Adam punches Blake in the face and Blake falls down. As Blake falls to the ground, he catches himself with both hands and kicks Adam's legs out from under him. Adam catches himself with one hand. Blake jumps up and step back. Adam pushes himself back up.

Adam: Seems to me like you are looking for something?
Blake: Yeah, you don't feel a lot of emotion do you?

Adam: Not while fighting, it's best to keep your head clear.
Blake: You are very good at that.
Adam: Thanks.

Adam jumps and roundhouse kicks Blake. Blake sees his opportunity and hits Adam in the chest. Adam's leg connects the same time as Blake's fist. They both fall to the floor.

Amusement.

Adam: Quite the gamble there.

Blake slowly pushes himself to a sitting position.

Blake: Did what I had to.
Adam: So you use other people's powers to fight?
Blake: Yeah. How did you know?
Adam: I do a lot of stuff around here. I hear the rumors.
Blake: I guess this place isn't any different than high school.

Anger.

Adam: There's a lot less drama than high school and the problems are actual problems.
Blake: Sorry.
Adam: It's alright. I've just worked in a lot of places and this is by far the best.
Blake: So how did you end up with S.T.A.T.E.?
Adam: I don't sleep, so I saw some stuff I wasn't supposed to.

Chapter 8

Blake: Don't sleep?
Adam: Nope.
Blake: You always been like that?
Adam: I used to sleep a little bit, but then I got in a huge accident and slept for a year. After I woke up, I never went back to bed.
Blake: Filled up your sleep meter.
Adam: (Laughs) I guess. You ready?
Blake: As I'll ever be.

Blake and Adam train for another hour before they are both barely standing.

Adam: I call that a good day.
Blake: You always beat your trainees bloody?
Adam: Only way I know how to train.

Adam walks over to a chair and closes his eyes.

Grant: Actually got him to sleep huh?

Blake looks over to see Grant at the door.

Blake: He said he didn't sleep.
Grant: He doesn't, unless he needs to heal.
Blake: Oh, what is he?
Grant: When you find out, let us know.
Blake: You don't know?
Grant: Nope, he's not like anything we've encountered.
Blake: That's cool.
Grant: So who sent you in here to train with Adam?
Blake: The Deputy Director.

Amusement.

Grant: What'd you do to tick her off?
Blake: I ticked her off?
Grant: Adam is usually the punishment for Junior Agents.
Blake: I can see why, but he was actually really helpful.
Grant: He's the best Multi-tool we have.
Blake: Multi-tool?
Grant: He does at least four different jobs here since he doesn't need to sleep.
Blake: Wow.
Grant: Now for the real reason I came in here.
Blake: What's that?

Grant walks up and places his hands on Blake's shoulders.

Grant: What are your intentions with Danielle?
Blake: That's not something I want to talk about.
Grant: I know her better than anyone here. If you can talk to anyone it's me.
Blake: Have you ever been near someone that you can't get close enough to?
Grant: I can't say I have.
Blake: I don't do the whole "feelings" thing. I just feel everyone else's. When I'm around her I can take on the entire world.
Grant: So you have no intentions of hurting her?
Blake: Not at all. I have never felt this way about anyone before.
Grant: Good. She feels strongly about you too.
Blake: I suppose relationships are discouraged here.

Chapter 8

Grant: You won't be able to be partners if you make Agent status, but other than that you'll be fine.
Blake: So I can ask where she is and stuff?
Grant: Yes, its better that you don't keep it a secret.
Blake: I still don't need everyone knowing.
Grant: They'll find out, they always do.
Blake: So where is she?
Grant: In the hallway.
Blake: Can I see her?

Grant signals toward the door. Blake heads to the door.

Grant: Hey Blake.
Blake: Yeah?
Grant: If you hurt her I will put enough ice shards into you that the ME will think you are hamburger.
Blake: Deal.

Blake walks outside the door and is greeted by a warm embrace. His entire body tingles.

Danielle: Why are you all beat up?
Blake: Apparently I ticked off the Deputy Director.
Danielle: What did you do?
Blake: I was trying to find you and got caught in a lie.
Danielle: (Laughs) What did you learn?
Blake: That Grant is protective and not to lie.
Danielle: You'd be better off. Feeling better?
Blake: Actually yeah.
Danielle: Your bruises are gone.
Blake: That's all thanks to you.
Danielle: (Smiles) You're welcome.
Blake: So what was your mission?

Danielle: Security for a magical item. They don't want Tomi to show up and take more stuff.
Blake: Sounds kind of boring.
Danielle: Ugh, it was!

Blake laughs.

Danielle: So did you hear that the other dogs are doing better?
Blake: That's good where are they?
Danielle: They're in Thane's lab.
Blake: Can we go see them.
Danielle: Sure let's go.

She grabs his hand and they walk briskly to a large metal door. *Tung! Tung!* Danielle knocks on the door. A man in a lab coat opens the door. Very thin framed glasses are barely visible on his face.

Man: Yes?
Danielle: Hi Thane, Blake would like to see the dogs.
Man: Ah Blake, yes they are here.

Blake holds out his hand.

Blake: Nice to meet you.
Thane: Nice to meet you as well.

Thane shakes his hand. They walk into the lab. The room is white and very clean. Three cages are sitting up against the wall. An island with a computer sits in the middle of the small room. There is a long hallway that leads out of the room, but it is not visible where

Chapter 8

it goes. The dogs occupy the cages. They stand upon seeing Blake.

Excitement. Excitement. Excitement.

Blake: Good to see you too.
Thane: They are much better without their less than capable handler.
Blake: Is that why he was so thin?
Thane: Yes. He was also controlling them in an unnatural fashion.

Thane types on a few keys and a 3-D image of Mitch appears next to his computer. He zooms up on Mitch's chest. Blood is leaking out of a bloody hole.

Blake: What is that?
Thane: He has had a very barbaric surgical procedure to replace his heart with that of a handler's.
Blake: Why would he do that?
Thane: Obviously he lacked the aptitude to control the dogs on his own, so he had to try another way.
Blake: Sounds desperate.
Thane: Speaking with him for more than a few moments proves that he has a definite need for gratification.
Blake: Explains why he tried to control three dogs at once.
Thane: A feat that has drained him and the beasts. Oddly enough, you had no problem controlling them.
Blake: Yeah.

Blake snaps his fingers and the dogs sit. Gauge appears in the room.

Surprise and Excitement.

Thane: That is impressive.

Thane walks up and looks over Gauge.

Thane: An unbound. He is so well mannered too.
Blake: Yeah, Gauge is pretty great.
Blake: How are you feeding them?
Thane: Our prisons are specially designed to sustain life energy. I boosted the levels and they responded very well.
Blake: How is Mitch doing?
Thane: He no longer needs to sustain these three so he is doing much better.

Blake kneels down and looks at the dog.

Blake: So the red on their bellies means they aren't unbound.
Thane: Yes. They are lesser versions of Gauge.
Blake: Lesser? What can Gauge do that they can't?
Thane: They cannot open portals on their own. They also have weaker minds and bodies. Their weak bodies limit their ability to grow more powerful and their weak minds limit their chance to rebel.
Blake: Makes them better servants.
Thane: Yes.
Blake: And since the unbound fight those that were once loyal to the Queen of Blood, they have to think on their own and be more powerful.

Chapter 8

Thane: It would appear you have learned a lot. Where did you get this information?
Blake: Mama Nancy.

Amusement.

Thane: I should've known. Has she told you her story?
Blake: No she hasn't.
Thane: It is an interesting one.
Blake: She usually only shares information with me when I press the issue.
Thane: Her life has not been an easy one. If you ever gain her trust, you will be the first in a very long time.
Blake: Good to know.
Thane: This next question is a personal one.
Blake: Ok.
Thane: Have there been any lingering effects from you using Markus' ability?
Blake: Not that I can think of.
Thane: You are very lucky.
Blake: I've been told.
Thane: Please excuse my intrusion.
Blake: It's no problem. Thanks for all the info.
Thane: You are welcome.

Danielle, Blake, and Gauge walk out of the lab. Gauge disappears.

Blake: Where's he going...

Warm lips press against his. His entire body tingles. Danielle pulls back and presses her forehead to his.

Danielle: Maybe he thought we should be alone.
Blake: He is pretty intuitive.

He wraps his arms around her and she does the same to him.

Danielle: Are you this way with all your girlfriends?
Blake: That's a roundabout way to ask if I've had any girlfriends.
Danielle: I've been told I'm too blunt.
Blake: You aren't. You are the first girl I have felt this way about.
Danielle: And what way are you feeling?

Blake kisses her.

Blake: Like I want to do that for the next forever.

Surprise. Joy.

Voice: No way!

Blake and Danielle look over to see Pulse and Scythe. Pulse hands Scythe a ten dollar bill.

Scythe: I told you.
Pulse: I didn't think the kid had the game to pull that off.

Danielle gives Blake a quick peck. Her hammer appears in her hand.

Danielle: Who wants to die first?

Chapter 8

Scythe: Pulse, he voted against you.

She slams the hammer in her hand. It disappears.

Danielle: You're not worth my time.

She hugs Blake.

Danielle: I'll see you later.
Blake: Ok.

She walks off.

Scythe: I knew that's why you were asking for Grant!
Blake: So you sent me to the Deputy Director!?
Scythe: Liars need to be punished.
Pulse: Agreed.
Blake: Hate you both.

Scythe and Pulse laugh.

Scythe: Ready to get going?
Blake: Yeah.
Scythe: I'll catch you later.
Pulse: Sure thing.

Scythe and Blake head to the car. They get in and head towards home.

Scythe: I'm glad you two found eachother.
Blake: So am I.
Scythe: I won't tell your dad, but you should.
Blake: I will, but not yet.

Scythe: Ok.

They arrive at home to see Rick in the kitchen and Jeff sitting on the couch. Blake heads to his room and lays down. The training with Adam took a lot out of him. His wounds are healed but there is a lingering soreness.

Frustration. Amusement. Surprise.

Blake steps out of his room and definitely smells smoke..

Jeff: Can't even make a grilled cheese!
Rick: Shut it Jeff.

Rick throws multiple black grilled cheese on the table.

Rick: Eat up.

Scythe and Blake sit down at the table.

Blake: I actually prefer them burnt.
Scythe: Food is food. It doesn't matter if it tastes good.
Rick: There we go.
Jeff: So I finally won, and I lose?
Rick: I'll work harder on yours.

Rick brings in a big bowl of tomato soup.

Rick: I didn't burn the soup.

Jeff takes a spoonful.

Chapter 8

Jeff: It's cold.

Surprise and anger.

Rick: Really!?
Jeff: No it's good.

Amusement. Relief and anger.

Rick: I'm dropping a car on you tomorrow.
Jeff: That is hurtful.

Blake and Scythe laugh. Blake feels a twinge of pain in his forehead.

Rick: What's up?
Blake: Not sure. I think there's something in the park.

Agony.

Blake falls out of his chair. Scythe catches him before he hits the floor. Blake shakes his head.

Blake: Definitely the park.
Rick: Be careful.
Blake: Always do.

Blake and Scythe run to the park to find a woman lying on the ground. She has long black hair that covers most of her body. Scythe calls for help on his phone. Blake and Scythe run over. Scythe picks her up. *Fwap!* She grabs his face. Boom! Blake kicks her in the chest and she flies off. Scythe's eyes roll into the back of his head. Thud! He hits the ground. Blake feels nothing from him. *Baboom!* Blake punches her in the face and she flies about twenty feet. She gets up and cracks her neck. She spits out a small amount of blood and runs off. Blake runs to Scythe and lays his head on Scythe's chest. He hears nothing.

CHAPTER 9

Anger and sadness well up in Blake as he feels for a pulse on Scythe and finds nothing.

Hunger.

Blake throws his arm behind him and connects with a soft object. It is the woman, and she flies back ten feet. Blake stands up and faces her. Her arm is awkwardly positioned. She pops it back into place.

Pain.

Blake: What did you do to my friend?

The woman rushes at him. He dodges to the side and punches her in the kidney. She crumples and skips off the ground. Blake falls to his knees and the world blurs.

How did I get so tired all of a sudden?

A black aura radiates from the woman as she works her way up to her hands and knees. She jumps up to her feet and blurs away.

Hunger.

Blake swings behind him and hits nothing.

Hunger.

She is now in front of him. *Fwap!* She grabs him by the neck and the world goes dark.

Worry and Anger. Fear.

A forest full of thick trees comes into view. Two people in camo and masks run up to Blake. They are holding large rifles with oddly shaped plastic containers on top of them.

This doesn't feel like me. It is familiar though.

They sit down and breathe heavily. One of them has the name "Anubis" printed on the back of their camo shirt.

Anubis: (Masculine voice) That was a bit hectic.
Other person: (More masculine voice) Decoy lost both his legs.

Anubis laughs.

Chapter 9

Anubis: You expect anything else Mike? He's still defending the flag too.
Mike: As many shots as he was taking, I was expecting him to be out for sure.

Blake: So what now?
Anubis: Right now it's four to eight. With Decoy guarding the flag, they are not going to get it.

Mike begins to laugh.

Anubis: What?
Mike: You think they'll ever learn not to shoot at the guy named Decoy?

Anubis laughs.

Anubis: They haven't learned yet.
Mike: Back to the plan.
Anubis: Alright, we play to our strengths. I'll draw fire, Mike cover me, and...
Mike: I wonder who's flanking!?
Anubis: I said play to our strengths.

Confidence wells up in Blake. Anubis, Mike, and Blake fist bump. Anubis drops his rifle and pulls out two pistols.

Anubis: You want my gun?
Blake: Not really fair if I have two.
Anubis: (chuckles) Good point.
Mike: Oh I got this.

Feelings of Power

Mike grabs the extra rifle. He props the stocks of each gun on his chest and nods. Anubis blurs off into a clearing. Loud popping sounds fill the woods. Multi-colored balls fly through the air at him. It is as if they are coming at him in slow motion. If a ball gets close, he gracefully moves out of its way. Mike stands up and lets out a courageous roar. *Popopopopopopopop!* Rapid fire pours out of Mike's rifles. Blake jumps and blurs through the woods. The enemy is way too focused on the two in the clearing. Blake is at their sides in moments. Pop! One to the mask. Pop! Pop! Pop! Two to the chest on one enemy and one to the head. Mike's rapid fire takes out two more defenders. Anubis blurs past Blake heading to a bright blue flag. Blake ducks into the trees and waits. Pop! Anubis barely dodges a shot going past his head. Pop! Blake makes the shooter pay with a shot to the mask. Anubis grabs the flag and bolts past Blake. Mike jumps behind and lays fire into the woods. *BEEP!* A horn blares. Everyone vanishes from the woods.

Voice: You have been very active the last couple days.
Blake: Oh mysterious voice, how I have missed you.

Amusement.

Voice: Are you trying to die?
Blake: Are you going to tell me who you are?
Voice: There are too many secrets in your world for me to tell you.
Blake: Well I'm not trying to die. I was trying to eat. Now...
Voice: You are worried about the one they call Scythe.

Chapter 9

Blake: I didn't feel anything from him.
Voice: Not typical for you.
Blake: No.
Voice: If he is as strong as you believe, he will be fine.
Blake: Do you know what she was?
Voice: I know who she was.
Blake: Who is she!?
Voice: What would life be if all the answers were given to you?
Blake: We're done, because I'm done talking to you.
Voice: We rarely get to speak.
Blake: And it doesn't get us anywhere!
Voice: Are you being entirely truthful?
Blake: No. You told me about connections and not to connect with Archdemons.

Pride and Joy.

Voice: See.
Blake: I'm sorry.
Voice: Apology accepted.
Blake: You're really not going to help me?
Voice: You are not ready for my help.
Blake: I guess I can understand that.

Joy.

VMMMM! A humming sounds fills Blake's ears. It feels like an elephant is sitting on his chest. He opens his eyes to a slightly purple ceiling. *Dadumdadum!* He feels his heartbeat in his ears. A migraine would be a welcome relief at this point. He looks around to see that he is in what looks like a prison cell.

Surprise and Excitement.

Payton: Blake's awake! Don't stand up.
Blake: Did she take my legs?
Payton: No, you're barely alive.
Blake: Is Scythe alive.

Sadness.

Payton: Barely.
Blake: Don't feel sad before you tell me if he's still alive.

Fear.

Payton: Sorry.

Blake falls out of bed and sits on the floor. His vision blurs in and out of focus.

Jane: Feels! What happened?
Blake: Apparently I'm not even allowed to have supper anymore.

Joy and sadness.

Jane: Do you know what it was?
Blake: The voice in my head wouldn't tell me.
Jane: You have voices now?
Blake: Voice, just one. Is Scythe going to make it?
Jane: He's unstable at the moment.

Blake struggles his way to his feet and slams up against the cell wall.

Chapter 9

Blake: Then let me after that woman.
Jane: Yeah right, you have to use everything you have to stand. How are you going to take on someone you couldn't beat when you were healthy?

Blake falls on his butt.

Blake: This is not a time for logic and reason. Let me see Scythe.
Jane: He's in the cell next to you.

Blake looks to his right and sees Gauge sitting in the cell wagging his tail.

Blake: Hey bud.
Jane: Other side.

Blake looks to his left to see Scythe in a hospital bed. The heart monitor next to Scythe shows a very low heart rate. He crawls over and lightly smacks the wall.

Blake: Wake up you idiot! If a weakling like me can survive, so can you!

Tears stream down Blake's face.

Blake: How are you supposed to protect me if you're being such a wuss!?

The heart rate increases slightly.

Surprise. Confusion.

Blake: That's what I thought.
Jane: Blake I need you to focus.
Blake: What?
Jane: What did the thing do that attacked you?
Blake: I felt a large amount of pain. We checked it out. She touched Scythe and put him down. I fought her for about fifteen seconds and now I'm here.
Jane: Did she say anything to you?
Blake: No.

Frustration.

Jane: Thank you.

Sara walks up and touches the wall.

Sara: What are you doing out of bed!?
Blake: Taking a walk.
Sara: Get back in there!
Blake: I don't have to listen to you.

Pulse and Grant walk up. Pulse lifts up Blake and puts him into bed.

Sara: Your vital signs are terrible, but they are much better than they were.

She covers Blake up.

Blake: Grant, where is Danielle?
Grant: She's passed out.
Blake: What happened?

Chapter 9

Pulse: She wrecked two training rooms when she saw you like this.
Blake: Oh. So she's mad?
Grant: She doesn't know how to handle it.
Blake: Oh.
Sara: You and Danielle? Cute. If you two want to become sexually active, you can always come to me for protection.

Surprise and embarrassment. Amusement. Amusement.

Blake feels his cheeks warm.

Blake: What...

Pulse and Grant laugh.

Pulse: Thank you Sara.
Sara: For what?
Pulse: Nothing, just thank you.
Sara: (Smiles) You're welcome.

Sara looks at Blake.

Sara: Stay in bed or I will find you.
Blake: Fine.

She steps out. Blake looks over at Gauge.

Blake: Why is Gauge in there?
Pulse: Multiple reasons. He was standing over you two when we found you. We thought he took you both out until Base played back what happened.

Feelings of Power

Blake: Ok? Why is he still in there?
Pulse: We figured you couldn't support him with being almost dead. We put him in there so you wouldn't have to.
Blake: Oh, thanks. Did you save me bud?

Pride.

Blake: Thanks, how are you still alive?

Gauge bares his fangs.

Blake: He bit her?
Pulse: On the arm, she freaked and ran.
Blake: I didn't even call him, that's awesome. Do you know who she is?
Pulse: No clue, we are working on developing a picture of her. Something about her is messing up even our cameras.
Blake: Ok. Do you know where she is?
Pulse: Heading north, no clue why.
Blake: Why aren't you after her?
Grant: You don't charge blindly into battle.
Blake: I do it all the time.
Pulse: And look where you are.
Blake: Good point.
Grant: Is there anything else you can think of?
Blake: She had some black aura around her.

Blake looks over at Scythe. The same black aura pulses around him.

Blake: Now it's on Scythe.

Chapter 9

Grant: You hear that Sara.
Sara: I'll check him out.

Sara opens the wall to Scythe's cell and put on gloves.

Pulse: How did she get into the park in the first place?
Blake: Didn't you have Base replay the scene?
Pulse: She couldn't go back that far, too much interference.
Blake: It felt similar to when Markus showed up.

Fear. Fear. Fear.

Payton: That's horrible.
Pulse: Forgot you were still here.

Irritation.

Payton: Thanks.
Pulse: So you're thinking a portal?
Blake: I would assume so.
Grant: Were you able to connect with her at all?
Blake: No. I did feel hunger and pain from her though.
Jane: This a good enough picture of her?

Jane throws a manila folder on Blake's lap. Blake pulls out the picture. It's a grainy, over the shoulder, picture of the woman.

Blake: A little grainy but that's her.
Jane: Thank you. Alright everyone, I have a meeting, get to your posts.

Everyone leaves except Sara who is looking at Scythe through an odd-looking pair of glasses.

I'm not staying cooped up in here.

Blake musters his energy and slides out of bed. He barely makes it out of the cell block before the doors close. He takes multiple deep breaths to stop his vision from blurring.

I'm fine if I don't move.

He catches glimpses of Pulse and the others.

I've got to talk to Grant to find out where Danielle is. She can make me feel better.

He sneaks behind Grant and Jane who are walking down a hallway he hasn't been in before.

Grant: Been a while since you were all in one place.
Jane: We are very busy. We don't have the time to meet every day and have coffee.
Grant: I wonder if they are dealing with similar problems.

Tsss! A snake appears in the hallway.

Fear.

Jane jumps back and stops abruptly. The snake vanishes.

Anger.

Chapter 9

Jane: Jasper!

Amusement.

A tall bearded man slowly fades into view. He is wearing a grey suit and is at least a foot taller than Jane. A big cheesy grin shows on his face.

Man: Hi!

Irritation.

Jane: Hello Jasper.
Jasper: You didn't have to throw yourself at me.
Jane: You're so lucky you don't work for me anymore.

Joy.

Jasper: Do you have a task to punish me? Those were always so fun!
Jane: Only you.
Grant: Hey Jasper, where's Bill?

Irritation.

Jasper: He's so slow!
Jane: He's hundreds of years old and falling apart.
Jasper: He's so slow!

An elderly looking man with gray skin walks into the hallway from the other side. Parts of his skin have bone showing through. He limps forward while using a cane.

Feelings of Power

Old Man: You telling everyone how I'm so slow Jasper?
Jasper: Not at all Bill. I was just telling them how lively you've been lately. I think you have another hundred years in this job.
Bill: I sure as hell hope not!
Voice: Sounds like someone needs a hug.

A large man with tan complexion walks down the hallway. He has short dark hair and a warm aura about him. He is followed by a tall bald man with slightly darker complexion. This man's face has no expression at all.

Bill: You even try to hug me Rich and I will beat you with my cane.
Bald Man: I'll snap your arm before you even touch him.
Jasper: Now now Dan, don't take you're protection duties too seriously.
Dan: You don't take them seriously enough.

Joy.

Blake focuses in Jasper's joy. His arm disappears in front of him. He looks at the rest of his body and it has vanished too.

Invisibility, that's a neat ability. I can't believe that worked first try.

Jane: Shall we.

Chapter 9

The wall opens up and all six walk into it. Blake follows in his new invisible state. The room is completely dark except for a single large table in the middle of the room. The six sit at the square table. Jane and Grant sit on one side. They are followed by Jasper and Bill who take up the second side. Rich and Dan take the third side. The fourth side is empty. *Tik! Tik! Tik!* A man in an entirely black suit walks into view. He has long, silver hair and a handlebar mustache.

Why doesn't he have a bodyguard?

Man: Welcome to the meeting.
Jane: It is good to see you Director.
Bill: It's been too long sir.
Rich: Seems like I just saw you yesterday.
Director: (Smiles) As our newest Deputy Director, I like to check in on you from time to time.
Rich: I figured.
Director: Let's get to business.

Blake sits on the floor in the dark.

Rich: Is it true you have Markus here?
Jane: Yes.
Bill: What!? I have a month left and you bring me to a place with an Archdemon!?
Jane: He is very secure.
Bill: He better be.
Rich: How did you manage to catch him alive?
Dan: Yeah, they call that guy "The Unbreakable".
Jane: We threw everything we had at him.

Jasper: I've heard it was one of your Junior Agents that took him out.

Anger. Surprise. Surprise. Disbelief. Surprise.

Jane: You heard wrong.

That kind of ticks me off.

Dan: Jasper is pretty good at collecting info.
Jane: Usually. As I said, it was a team effort. There were a few Junior Agents that assisted in the fight.

Jane shoots a glare at Jasper.

Director: Doesn't really matter how it happened, the fact is that it did.
Rich: I just have a question for Jane.
Jane: What?
Rich: There has been an Agent blacked out in multiple reports as of late. What are you hiding?
Jane: I am following protocol. "If you fear for the safety of any person, place, or thing, their identity may remain confidential in all reports".
Director: Understood. Is this answer good enough?

Fear.

Rich: You're talking like we're in a time of war.
Jane: We very well might be.
Bill: She does have a point. If Markus is waltzing into one of our bases, this is not a normal time.

Chapter 9

Excitement.

Jasper: I can't wait to find out who mister or misses mysterious is.
Director: Jane, can you give more information on what has been happening in your section?
Jane: We've had multiple demonic portals open up. A known demon contact was killed by Ronaldo and Rachel. The EoL has been more active than normal. I also have an Agent in the hospital from an unknown assailant.
Jasper: Which Agent?
Jane: Scythe.

Surprise and Anger. Anger.

Jasper: Any info on this assailant?

Jane tosses the picture on the table.

Surprise and Anger. Fury and Sadness.

Dan: I know who that... woman is.
Jane: Who is she?
Dan: The Skinwalker that took my baby girl.
Rich: If that's true, she also took at least six other children.
Jane: How have I not heard of this?
Dan: It happened almost sixteen years ago.
Jane: What ever happened to her?
Dan: S.T.A.T.E. pursued her for five years and then she suddenly vanished.
Jane: So she's a Skinwalker?

Grant: I'll let Sara know. Excuse me.

Blake tucks in the corner as Grant walks past.

Jane: Thank you.
Dan: Where is she now?
Jane: Last we saw her, she was heading north.
Dan: Do you have anyone pursuing her?
Jane: I didn't even find out what she was until now.

Fury.

Dan stands up.

Dan: So you just let her run around on her own!?

Anger.

Jane stands up.

Jane: I'm not sending my people in blind!
Dan: You don't know what this woman is capable of!
Jane: The very reason we didn't pursue her.
Director: That is enough. Return to your seats.

Dan and Jane sit.

Jasper: Jane made the right choice.

Annoyance.

Dan: Imagine, you would take her side.

Chapter 9

Jasper: I'm taking the side of common sense. You don't go after a werewolf without silver or a demon without some iron. If we don't know how to fight something, it's just relying on blind luck to survive.
Dan: Well now you know what she is.
Jane: And I have a team already in mind.

Grant returns and sits down. He leans over to whisper to Jane. Blake crawls on the floor to listen in.

Grant: (Whisper) Sara needs to analyze the Skinwalker to ensure Scythe recovers. Blake's missing.

Irritation.

Jane: (Whisper) Then we need to detain her as soon as possible. Blake's probably looking for his girl.
Grant: (Whisper) Agreed on the Skinwalker. Cameras show Blake turning invisible in the hallway with us. I think he's in here.

Oops. Amusement. Wait she's not mad?

Jane: (Whispering) Crafty little brat.
Jasper: What's up?
Grant: Our Doc thinks she has a way to patch up Scythe.
Jasper: That's good. We'd have quite the vengeful spirit if he dies.
Director: That is excellent news. Is there any other business?
Jasper: Queen Yayouya is missing.
Rich: How do you lose a seventy year old woman with lung cancer?

Jasper: She put some illusion up that we were not prepared for.
Jane: I though magic was too much for her now?
Jasper: It was, but she must've had a reason to try.

Curiosity fills the room.

Director: Every section will be placed on high alert. There is too much going on that we do not have contained.

Everyone nods.

Rich: We have an issue as well.

Rich slides manila folders to Bill and Jane. Blake peaks over her shoulder. Jane pulls out pictures of an Asian boy with short white hair and a Latino boy with a black two inch Mohawk.

Jane: Who are they and what did they do?
Dan: They slaughtered everyone at a backwoods bar near the border of Sections 2 and 1.
Jasper: How?
Dan: The Latino kid beat them to death and the Asian kid stabbed his victims through the heart.
Jane: Who are they?
Rich: From what Racquet could see of their abilities, we believe they are the sons of Narkis and Elias.

The room is filled with surprise and fear.

Jasper: Just to clarify, the Archdemons?

Chapter 9

Dan: You know anyone else with idiotic names like that?

Irritation and Amusement. Anger.

Jasper: Just clarifying.
Bill: Where are you getting your information? We've always been told that Archdemons are infertile.

Rich types on the table in front of him. A 3-D image of the boys appears in the middle of the table. The Asian boy's arms have white marks that look like bones etched on his skin. The marks grow and turn into a bony exoskeleton. The Latino boy grows two feet and his muscles expand.

Jasper: So they have their father's abilities?
Bill: They could just be high-ranking soldiers in their armies. We shouldn't jump to the conclusion that they are Archdemon children.
Director: Bill is right. Although this conclusion could be made, we must not assume. They will need to be detained for questioning.
Rich: We lost track of them but are continuing to search.
Director: So Osric is the only one to not make an appearance as of late.
Bill: Diane too.
Jasper: Incorrect sir. Jane's reports speak of demon dogs which are pets of Diane.
Director: Correct Jasper, good job.
Bill: Must've missed that email...

Grant: Actually, Skinwalkers fall under Osric's jurisdiction. Normally I wouldn't say he's involved, but look at the other evidence.
Director: So the Archdemons are making a play. Anyone know what it is?
Jasper: They rarely, if ever, work together; it has to be something big.
Jane: That's true, they hate each other for the most part. We all need to keep our eyes peeled for anything that could be a clue.
Director: Due to the circumstances, any Agent on solo work will return to their bases or be assigned a partner. We need to keep everyone safe during these times.

Everyone nods.

Director: Due to the emotions behind the Skinwalker, Section 3 will form a team to pursue her.

Surprise and Anger.

Jane: Sir, my teams are more than qualified.
Director: Scythe is liked by almost your entire Section. I cannot afford someone to become overzealous and lose us valuable information.
Jane: Can we at least hold her?
Director: For what purpose?
Jane: To aid in Scythe's care. It would be nice to have easy access to the type of ability that hurt him.
Director: I do not believe that would be the best course of action. Section 3 will capture, question, and detain the Skinwalker.

Chapter 9

Anger and Worry.

Jane: Understood.

The Director fades away. Rich and Dan exit the room followed by Jasper and Bill. The door closes.

Jane: One...Two...

Blake jumps up.

Blake: I'm here, I'm here.

Joy.

Jane: What makes you think you can listen in on our conversation?
Blake: I was able to sneak in here with little to no effort?
Jane: You are suspended.
Blake: What does that mean?
Jane: It means you'll be escorted home and resume your normal life until told otherwise.
Blake: Oh alright.

Grant escorts Blake out to a black SUV and drives him home in silence. Upon arrival, Blake steps out of the vehicle.

Blake: So what do I do now?
Grant: Now would be a great time to catch up with some friends to take your mind off of your predicament.
Blake: Ok.

Feelings of Power

Blake walks into the house and is greeted by a big hug.

Rick: I'm so glad you are alright. How's Scythe?
Blake: He's not even stable
Rick: I'm sorry son.
Blake: It's alright. I got suspended too.
Rick: What did you do?
Blake: Listened to a conversation I wasn't supposed to.
Rick: Well sounds like your fault.
Blake: Yeah. I'm too tired to worry about it. At least I have the whole weekend to figure stuff out.
Rick: Not really, it's 9PM on Saturday.
Blake: I was out for almost a whole day?
Rick: Yeah.
Blake: Ugh… it's time for bed.
Rick: Let me know if you need anything kiddo.
Blake: Will do.

Blake goes into his room and lays down.

Why was Jane happy before she suspended me?

Blake winces from pain in his head and body. He lays down his head and goes to bed.

CHAPTER 10

Jane: Feels, wake up.

Blake jumps up to find Jane and a woman with long red hair in his room. He holds his head in his hands.

Blake: I thought you suspended me.
Jane: That's because I would never ask an Agent to disobey orders.
Blake: What?

Worry.

Jane: I need you to capture the Skinwalker.
Blake: And how am I supposed to do that?
Jane: You're a resourceful kid and you know what you are up against now.
Blake: By myself.
Jane: I can't give you any help from anyone in my command.
Blake: So no help.

Sadness.

Jane: I also can't protect you if the Director comes after you.
Blake: And no backup.
Jane: I wouldn't ask unless I had to.
Blake: You don't have faith in Section 3?
Jane: They'll capture her, I just don't know how much time it will take.
Blake: And we don't know how much time Scythe has.
Jane: No, thus the reason I'm even asking you to do this in the first place.

Blake jumps out of bed and shakes his head.

Blake: Can I have Gauge?
Jane: His cell may or may not be able to stop him from transporting himself to you.
Blake: If I call him now they will see something is up.
Jane: Now you're thinking.
Blake: I'll do it.

Joy and Worry.

Jane: Don't go dying on me.
Blake: Scythe won't get better if I do.
Woman: The window is closing.
Jane: I need to go.
Blake: I gotcha.

Jane and the woman leave out his bedroom door.

Chapter 10

Blake: No time like the present.

Blake changes clothes and takes a look at the clock.

6AM, that's a good chunk of sleep.

He sneaks out the front door and heads down the street.

Only one place I can get backup now.

He arrives at Mama Nancy's house and knocks on the door. Shane answers the door.

Shane: What's up?
Blake: I need your help.
Shane: With?
Blake: I need to capture a Skinwalker.
Shane: Why are you messing with one of those?
Blake: It hurt Scythe.
Shane: Why isn't S.T.A.T.E. helping you?
Blake: I got suspended.

Amusement.

Shane: Nice, come on in.
Blake: Thanks.

There is quite the congregation in Mama Nancy's living room. An elderly woman with dark complexion is sitting on the couch with Mama Nancy. A fit woman with short brown hair leans in the door way to the living room. A large man sits behind the elderly woman. He has glasses, short dark hair, and a goatee.

Woman: What do you want?
Blake: Help.
Man: This really isn't the place for that.

Blake looks at the woman. She is sporting a fur vest that looks familiar.

Blake: I don't have anywhere else to go.
Elderly Woman: Is this the empath?
Mama: Yes it is.

Curiosity. I'm curious who you are too lady.

The woman stands up and squares her body with Blake's. Her nails extend and turn black. Blake blurs forward and pushes her into the wall.

Surprise. Amusement.

She swings her arms and he jumps back.

Elderly Woman: Aha! He actually caught you off guard Zara.

Joy. I know exactly who you are now.

Zara: I see that.

Worry and Anger.

Mama: Don't wreck my house!

Chapter 10

Zara signals to the back door and Blake follows her into the backyard. The backyard is open with a tall fence blocking the view of the curious.

Zara: Stephen.
Man: It's already up.

Zara and Blake square off. Goosebumps cover Blake's body as adrenaline flows through his veins. Zara blurs in and brings her claws down on Blake. *THUD!* His forearm stops the progress of her arm. *Thud!* His fist connects with her stomach. *Squish!* Her claws sink into his punching arm. He brings his other hand and wraps it around her hand. Her claws sink deeper into his arm. *BAM!* He brings his knee into her stomach and jumps on her back. He pushes her to the ground and jumps back. She jumps back up and shows off a mouth full of fangs. Blood rushes down Blake's hand but only for a moment. The gaping holes in his arm shrink and disappear. Blake blurs behind Zara and slams her into the ground. She springs back up and kicks him into the ground.

She's quick.

Elderly Woman: That's enough.

Disappointment.

Zara walks up and holds her hand out to Blake.

Blake: Thanks.

He grabs it and she pulls him up.

Zara: You actually made this job less boring.
Blake: So are you Rachel's sister?

Surprise.

Zara: How do you know Rachel?
Blake: I watched her kill a bunch of people.
Zara: That sounds like her and yes I am.
Blake: I thought so, you look a lot alike.

The elderly woman coughs loudly into her hand. *Drip! Drip!* Blood drips from her hand. Stephen walks over and hands her a rag.

Elderly Woman: Thanks.
Blake: Shot in the dark, Queen Yasomethingorother?

Amusement. Surprise. Surprise. Pride.

Elderly Woman: Yayouya and yes. How do you know of me?
Blake: From a conversation I wasn't supposed to hear.
Yayouya: I see. Are you going to report me?
Blake: I'm suspended and have no reason to do that. Oh that reminds me, I need help.
Mama: Help with what?

Shane, Steve, and Monique step out of the house.

Shane: Got any tips for capturing a Skinwalker?
Mama: Don't try to capture a Skinwalker?

Chapter 10

Yayouya: Now why would you be looking to play with a Skinwalker?
Blake: She hurt my friend.
Yayouya: So it is vengeance you seek.
Blake: Not really, I need her to make him better.
Yayouya: I see. Skinwalkers are hurt by the purest of nature. White Ash and White Oak weapons are the most effective. Against the one you seek, a bow would be the best weapon.
Blake: I bet Zara could hurt her.

Pride. Amusement.

Yayouya: Yes, her claws would penetrate the Skinwalker aura, but she cannot join you.
Blake: So what if I just hit her really hard?
Yayouya: Most physical damage is completely ineffective against such beasts.
Shane: We've got this.

Steve is holding a large bag.

Blake: Nice, let's go.
Mama: You just can't take my kids.
Blake: You have Mark and Taylor.
Yayouya: And we will stay here until nighttime.

Joy.

Mama: Don't die.
Shane: We won't.

They walk behind the house to a large shed. Shane opens the door to reveal a large jeep.

Steve: Can you feel her out?
Blake: Yeah.

Monique touches Blake's neck.

Monique: She is very powerful.

Excitement. Excitement. Excitement.

Blake: You are all excited?
Shane: Haven't had a good fight since you beat us in the street.

Irritation.

Monique: It won't happen again.
Shane: Oh no, we know what we're up against now.

Blake smiles.

Blake: You guys are awesome.
Shane: Why?
Blake: I don't know anyone else who would be so gung ho to join me in battle.
Shane: Meh, we're just bored. Plus you owe me tungsten marbles.
Steve: I want two hook swords, the monk style.
Monique: You two are childish.
Shane: I'm not saying I have to have them, just saying it would be nice.

Chapter 10

Monique: Sure.

They all jump into the jeep. The jeep starts up and rumbles the shed. Shane pulls out and they head out.

Shane: Where to?
Blake: Last I heard, she was heading north. Stick as close to the woods as possible. I'm assuming that's where she'll be hiding.
Shane: Done.

Blake scans the area and spots the tiniest flicker of black. He points and Shane takes the jeep off road. They travel for 20 minutes before they find a large gathering of the black aura. Blake jumps out and walks to a nearby cave.

Blake: She's not here.
Monique: She must've stopped to rest here.

Blake tastes copper and walks further into the cave. A dead deer resides in the cave. It is missing all of the fur on its back.

Monique: Was she hungry?

Ting! Steve barely blocks a rack of horns from running him through. Shane throws two sticks and Steve catches them. *Whap! Whap!* He strikes the deer in the neck and the snout. It falls to its front legs and jumps back up. Blake sees the black aura pouring off of it.

Blake: Pretty sure it's her.

Shane: They don't call them Skinwalkers for nothing.

She blurs away.

Shane: Let's move.

They hop back in the jeep and follow the black aura. The Skinwalker is running in the ditches. Shane is keeping up with her. Shane lets go of the wheel and pulls a wooden stake out of the bag. He sends it rocketing at her. *Tatik!* She turns and knocks it away with her horns. *Thud!* Shane kicks Steve out of the passenger seat. Blake grabs Monique and jumps up. *Kaboom!* The jeep crashes into the Skinwalker. A blur leaves the wreckage and runs away.

Shane: I hope that's covered by my insurance.

Hmm...

Blake blurs after her.

Ok, how am I still connected to Zara?

He catches up to the Skinwalker. She is running straight at a large boy with dark complexion. She picks up speed.

Blake: Watch out! Don't let her touch you.

Fear.

Chapter 10

The boy catches the Skinwalker by her horns and throws her to the side. She jumps out of the deer's skin and lunges at the boy. *Baboom!* She flies off into the woods. The boy's hands are black as coal with glowing red cracks in them.

Fear.

Boy: What is that thing?
Blake: Not anything you want to mess with.

The growth around the Skinwalker turns black and she steps out of the woods.

Skinwalker: Abomination!

She blurs at the boy. Blake catches her by the throat.

Skinwalker: (Smirks) Didn't you learn last time boy.
Blake: A little different circumstances this time.

Blake squeezes her throat tighter. His hands are black as coal. She kicks off his chest and goes for his throat. She catches a staff instead. *Thwap!* A bat connects with her stomach. She rips the staff away jumps back. *Tsss!* The staff appears to burn her hands. She drops it.

Skinwalker: You do not know what you are protecting.
Blake: You don't know why we're here!

Blake runs at her with Steve and Monique. Monique slides and grabs her staff. Steve comes from above with the bat. *Bam!* Blake punches the Skinwalker in the chest. The grass underneath the Skinwalker dies. She lunges at Steve. Shane appears and sticks her in the shoulder with a stake. *Fwap!* She grabs his throat and his body goes limp. Blake brings his fists down on the Skinwalker.

Intense fury.

Monique grabs the Skinwalker by the throat and touches Shane. *Carack!* The Skinwalker and Monique fall to the ground. Shane jumps up to his hands and knees and gasps for air.

Boy: What the....

Steve walks up and checks Monique's pulse.

Steve: She'll be ok. How you feeling Shane?

Shane shakes his head and gives a thumbs up.

Shane: Safe to say... any fight I had left in me... is gone now.

Steve pulls a net out of the bag and wraps up the Skinwalker. Blake walks up to the boy.

Blake: Who are you?
Boy: My name is Damion.
Blake: Nice to meet you. You better get out of here.
Damion: Ok.
Blake: Not to be weird, but if you have anywhere to go that isn't in this state, you would be safer there.

Chapter 10

Damion: Thank you.

Damion runs off.

The coal on Blake's hands disappears.

You better not be who I think you are.

Shane: I'm assuming S.T.A.T.E. felt all that.
Blake: More than likely.

Steve picks up all their weapons. Shane struggles to his feet and walks over to Monique.

Shane: We're getting out of here.
Blake: How?
Steve: We have two feet.

Shane and Steve throw one arm of Monique's on each of their shoulders and walk off. Blake walks over to the Skinwalker and sits down.

She's still breathing.

Suddenly Grant, Base, Pulse, and Thane appear in the grass.

Grant: Blake get on the ground!
Blake: I'm already sitting.

Voom! A bubble of rippling air flies at him and he barely is able to lay down to dodge it.

Blake: I'm down.

Grant flips Blake over and puts cuffs on him.

Anger.

Thud! Blake is punched in the gut by Pulse.

Pulse: What gives you the right to throw away your life like this!?

Blake coughs. Thane walks over to the Skinwalker and a coffin size barrier appears around her.

Thane: She should be safe to transport now.
Pulse: How did you even do this?
Blake: Sorry, I was too busy getting punched to respond to you!

Anger.

Rippling air appears around Pulse's fist. It quickly dissipates. Base teleports everyone and Blake is thrown hard into his cell.

Thane: I will get to work on this immediately.

Thane and Grant walk out.

Pulse: Going after the Skinwalker when you're suspended! You're never going to be an agent now.

Blake gets up and locks eyes with Pulse.

Chapter 10

Blake: While you were sitting here following orders, I was out there saving Scythe.

Fury.

Rippling air wraps around both of Pulse's hands and dissipates as he walks away. Sara is still in Scythe's cell. She walks out and into Blake's cell. *Whack!* She slaps him in the face.

Blake: You too?
Sara: Simply checking reflexes Blake. Lay down.

Blake lays in his bed. Sara looks at him with her weird glasses on.

Confusion.

She pulls out a scalpel and cuts Blake's arm.

Blake: Ouch, what?

She grabs a pair of tweezers and pulls out a black claw. It bursts into dust.

Sara: What was that?

Zara's claw? Explains how I was still connected to her. Also explains my cockiness. I'm going to have to apologize to Pulse.

Blake: A sliver? I don't know.

Sara: Uh huh. You're fine.

She walks out and leaves.

Excitement.

Blake looks over to see Gauge sitting and his tail wagging. Blake kneels down and looks at Gauge.
Blake: Really wish I could've brought you with bud.

Gauge puts his paw on the cell. Blake puts his hand on the other side.

Tik! Tap! Tik! Rapid foot prints walk up Blake's cell. It is Jane.

Jane: So because we weren't going to capture her, you had to do it yourself?
Blake: Yep.
Jane: And you think this will go unpunished?
Blake: Not at all. Anything is better than sitting here doing nothing.
Jane: The Director has been notified and is figuring out your punishment. It is out of my hands.
Blake: Understood.

Joy.

Jane: You're lucky to be alive.
Blake: I know.
Jane: At least you have that.

Chapter 10

Jane walks away. Danielle walks up.

Joy. Hmm.., only joy? I was expecting some anger from that.

Danielle opens the door. Blake cowers.

Blake: I'm sorry.

Amusement.

Danielle: Why are you so scared?
Blake: I figured you'd be mad.
Danielle: That all depends, are you going to do that again?
Blake: Not really a chance to. I don't think I will be an agent anymore.
Danielle: Good.

She hugs him and squeezes him tightly. He wraps his arms around her and kisses her. They sit on the bed together.

Blake: You're really not mad?
Danielle: (Whispering) I was on my way to get you so we could get her, but you already left.
Blake: What?
Danielle: (Smirks) I would've done the same thing.
Blake: So what happens if I'm not an agent anymore?

Danielle gets up and kisses him on the head.

Danielle: Since I'll be the career woman, you get to stay at home and watch the kids.

Blake: Kids?
Danielle: You aren't getting away from me.
Blake: (Smiles) You are the best.

She walks out of his cell and blows him a kiss. He smiles and she walks away.

Worry. Just a flicker, but I knew she was hiding something.

He lays his head on his pillow. *Vmmm!* All of the lights turn off.

Voice: Now now, how did they manage this?

Blake is filled with an overwhelming sense of fear. *Vmmm!* The lights turn back on. Blake looks around. Gauge is still wagging his tail. He closes his eyes to see what he can feel.

Exhaustion. Curiosity.

He opens his eyes, but there is still no one around.

Blake: You see anything Gauge?

Gauge tilts his head and wags his tail.

Blake: (Smirks) So helpful.

At least I probably don't have to go to school tomorrow... But I'm curious about Shane and the others!

Chapter 10

He closes his eyes.

Tung! Tung! Someone knocks on his cell wall. Blake opens his eyes and looks around. Grant is there to greet him.

Blake: What time is it?
Grant: Time for you to go to school.
Blake: You sure I won't run?
Grant: You'll only look guiltier if you do.
Blake: True.

Grant escorts Blake out to the car and takes him to school.

Grant: Be here right after school.
Blake: I have cheerleading practice.

Anger.

Grant looks at Blake with no emotion.

Grant: Funny.

Grant pulls away.

Disappointment. Who is that from?

Rick is standing behind him.

Blake: Hey dad.
Rick: So what did you do?

Blake: I went to get that girl that hurt Scythe to save him.

Pride.

Rick: At least you had a good reason. How are you doing?
Blake: I have no idea how to feel to tell you the truth. I'm proud of myself for capturing the Skinwalker. I'm disappointed that I'm under trial for doing it. I'm sad that Scythe doesn't look any better. I'm curious and more than a little scared of what they are going to do to me.
Rick: You think they'll hurt you?
Blake: No, but that's just it, I have no idea what they are going to do.
Rick: Well you did what you thought was right.
Blake: I did.
Rick: If they punish you for that, they aren't the good guys they claim to be.
Blake: Yeah.
Rick: So what part of what you did was wrong?
Blake: I listened to stuff I wasn't supposed to and went after the Skinwalker when someone else was supposed to.
Rick: You did what they couldn't, that's not your fault. I'm not going to defend you for being nosy.
Blake: (Smiles) I wouldn't expect you too.
Rick: You still have a home even if they kick you out.
Blake: Best home there is.

Blake hugs Rick.

Chapter 10

Rick: Now get going. You don't want to be late.
Blake: Thanks Dad.
Rick: I may not get all this Skinwalker and S.T.A.T.E. business, but I will always be here for you.
Blake: I'm sorry if it's rough on you.
Rick: It's what you sign up for when you become a dad.
Blake: I didn't know there was a supernatural defense clause in your father contract.
Rick: Really fine print. I'll see you when you get this all sorted out.
Blake: Sure thing.

Blake heads into school. Shane, Steve, and Monique are absent.

I hope they're ok.

The school day goes by like any other day. Blake is walking to his next class when he is pulled aside.

Zara: How's it going?
Blake: Good, what are you doing here?
Zara: Just wanted you to know that all of Mama's bodyguards are well and resting.
Blake: (Smiles) Thanks, I was worried about them.

Zara gets really close to Blake's face and he backs away.

Blake: What are you doing?
Zara: Nothing, why?
Blake: You were just getting very close to me.
Zara: Are you scared of me?
Blake: No, I think you are awesome.

Joy.

Zara: Then what's the problem.
Blake: I have a girlfriend.

Disappointment.

Zara: I thought I smelled an odd scent on you.
Blake: Yeah she's pretty unique.

Zara puts her hand on Blake's cheek.

Zara: If you are ever looking for something a bit wilder than a little hybrid, I'll be around.

She blurs away.

What!? Now do I tell Danielle about that? Is she better off not knowing? Am I a jerk for hiding it? As if I didn't have enough to worry about.

The rest of the day is filled with Blake arguing in his own head. He meets up with Grant after school.

Grant: How was school?
Blake: Oh just another typical day full of no events.
Grant: Sounds fun.

They drive off and arrive at S.T.A.T.E. Grant hands Blake a nice suit.

Blake: What is this for?
Grant: You need to look presentable.

Chapter 10

Blake: Ok.

Blake heads into a bathroom and puts on the suit.

And so it begins.

He walks out and is escorted to a large room. There are about thirty people sitting in row of chairs. In front of the chairs is a wall with a single chair sitting in the middle of the room. In front of the single seat sits three raised tables with a fourth table raised above them. He is escorted to the single seat by Pulse. He sits and waits. He does his best to maintain his cool with all these people in one room.

I'll find out what he's thinking.
What?
Wait, you can hear me?
Fear. Yeah, what are you doing in my head?
What are you doing in my head!

Blake looks around and sees a young man with glasses staring at him.

You done staring at me?
I will find out what you are hiding and notify the Director.
You want to know what I'm hiding?

Blake thinks back.

Voice: Let's just see if that which you are so proud of can save you. Unrelenting pain.

Sweat pours down the young man's face. He passes out. The people around him rush to his aid. They take him out of the courtroom.

Blake returns to his waiting.

The Director and each of the Deputy Directors walk in and sit in front of Blake. The Director sits at the highest table. Dan, Jasper, and Grant walk in after and sit next to their Deputy Directors.

Director: Now Blake, what are we going to do with you?

Booom! Two of the room's doors fly in and off their hinges.

CHAPTER 11

Baboom! The doors to the room fly open.

Voice: Do I get to say anything about all this?

Scythe walks into the room with Sara hanging off his arm.

Sara: You are nowhere near the condition to be up and about, you need to go back.
Director: Scythe, I'm glad you have made such a great recovery.

Sara stands in front of the Director.

Sara: He is not recovered enough to be moving around.
Director: Have you recovered enough to stand and speak Scythe?
Scythe: Yes I have sir.

Sara walks back into the crowd and sits down.

Director: Good. Now what do you have to say?
Scythe: I hear Blake is here because he did something to try and save me.
Director: That is partially the truth.
Scythe: Well he better not be in trouble for trying to save a fellow agent.
Director: He knew that Section 2 was going to be handling the capture of the Skinwalker that hurt you.
Scythe: How?
Director: My sources tell me that he eavesdropped on a meeting I was having with the Directors.

Irritation.

Scythe looks at Blake.

Scythe: Really?

Blake hangs his head in shame.

Scythe: I didn't know that. That doesn't change the fact that he was trying to save me and I am grateful for that.

Scythe walks up and sits on the floor next to Blake.

Director: We are also thankful to Blake for saving you Scythe. We just do not believe the way he did it was the best course of action for his safety or of the safety of those around him. Now the question is, did you act alone?
Blake: No I didn't but I did not work with anyone from S.T.A.T.E.

Chapter 11

Director: So you didn't receive orders from anyone within S.T.A.T.E?
Blake: Not that I'm aware of.
Director: Explain.
Blake: This is a secret agency. I have no idea who could be working for S.T.A.T.E.

Amusement.

The director laughs.

Director: Excellent point. Who did you work with?
Blake: I'd rather not say sir.
Director: Are they, as far as you know, wanted by S.T.A.T.E?
Blake: No.
Director: Ok. Now let's address the safety issue you presented yourself with.
Scythe: He's still alive, that's proof enough that he was safe.
Director: It could be seen like that. It could also be seen as dumb luck.
Scythe: Well then test him.
Director: How?
Scythe: Give him the field agent test.

Shock. Anger.

Jane: He can't take that test.
Dan: No kidding, I haven't even heard of this kid til today.
Director: They are correct, that is not a test for someone as new to S.T.A.T.E. as Blake.

Feelings of Power

Scythe: The test measures skill, not seniority.
Director: I like your proposition. Why not give it a whirl?

Surprise fills the room.

Jane: Sir, that is not fair to my other Junior Agents who have been here longer and put more effort in.
Director: I don't believe that you and I are on the same page. Blake is not fighting to become an Agent.
Jane: Ok?
Director: If this were simply a case of a Junior Agent going out on their own, it could be the case that they would be tested in this way. Blake made this much more complicated. Being that he disobeyed almost direct orders, he will be fighting to remain a Junior Agent.

Anger.

Jane: Seems justifiable.
Rich: So how is this going to go down?
Director: Blake and his team must win to prove he is skilled enough to have not endangered himself in this mission.
Jane: How many rounds do they have to win?
Director: As many as it takes?
Jane: Ok?
Jasper: Usually it's a grading scale and winning is extra points.
Director: This is not a usual situation.
Jasper: Understood.
Director: Do Section 2 and 3 have their teams ready?
Bill: You mean right now?

Chapter 11

Director: I have many things to do. I also lack the patience to wait and see what happens next.
Jasper: We can have them ready in an hour.
Director: Rich?
Rich: That's enough time for us.
Director: Then it is settled. You have an hour to get ready Blake.
Blake: I don't even know what I'm getting ready for.
Director: You are running out of time to figure it out. Oh and one last thing. Blake's team will be down a person.
Jane: Why?
Director: I need to ensure he is pulling his weight.

Anger.

Jane: Ok.

Blake and Scythe are walked into a large round room with tons of plastic-looking weapons and armor adorning the walls. Jane walks in and begins pacing back and forth.

Jane: Ok Blake, you get to pick one agent for the challenge.
Blake: Scythe, if you're up for it?

Anger.

Jane: He can't even move.
Scythe: I can move.

Irritation.

Jane: You were almost dead.
Scythe: Almost doesn't count.

Jane rubs her forehead.

Jane: I will be monitoring your vitals. If they slip for a second, I will pull you out of there!
Scythe: Deal.
Jane: Ok, you get to pick two other Junior level agents or lower.
Scythe: Where is Riley at in his training?
Jane: He's actually only the field test away from completing his test.
Scythe: Riley it is.
Jane: Now you need one more.
Blake: Danielle.
Jane: She's already an Agent.
Blake: I didn't know that.
Scythe: Yeah, she's the youngest person to pass the test.
Blake: Hmm...
Scythe: You are not replacing me with her.
Blake: Come on Scythe, you're almost dead.
Scythe: I'll show you almost dead.
Jane: Quit it. Feels, I am not going to let you get distracted by having Danielle here.
Blake: I thought you said I get to choose?
Jane: You did.

Amusement.

Scythe smiles.

Chapter 11

Jane: Payton and Cody have passed their tests as well.
Blake: What about Adam?

Excitement. Sadness.

Jane: He is qualified but he only took the other tests because he was bored and couldn't sleep.
Blake: He's good.
Jane: Grant, go ask him.
Grant: Yes ma'am.
Blake: I didn't even see him in here.
Scythe: Me either.

Thane enters the room.

Jane: Strip down to your boxers.
Blake: Are you going to leave?
Jane: You don't have anything I haven't seen before.
Blake: Yeah cause they're all the same.

Scythe strips down to his boxers and stands up. Thane hands him what looks like a scuba suit. As he pulls it on, it appears to adhere to his skin. It covers all of his body except for his face. Thane is holding a tablet. Scythe's outline appears on the tablet's screen.

Thane: Everything is looking normal.
Blake: What is it?
Thane: These suits are designed to limit the power output of the wearer. They also monitor vitals and provide fairly adequate protection. The suit also disables itself where an injury takes place.
Blake: What?

Jane: They keep you safe and shut down if you take too much damage.
Blake: Thanks.

Thane hands Blake a suit. As he puts it on, the cool material bonds to his skin. It warms and Blake can't even feel it on his skin.

Blake: That's cool.
Thane: You have been provided with basic armor and weapons that you would wear in the types of situations

Scythe puts on a full set of black gear.

Thane: These sets contain a bullet proof vest and helmet. All the clothes are reinforced to take extra damage.
Blake: Nice. Wait, bullet proof?
Jane: People have guns Blake.
Blake: If we don't kill people, why do we have guns?
Jane: Your enemies will have guns. We use guns to shoot non-lethal rounds at those we need to capture. You need to learn that guns can't kill everything.
Blake: Ok?

Blake puts on a set of black clothes as well. Riley walks into the room with Adam.

Adam: This is a lot more fun than I had planned for the day.
Jane: This is not a game Adam.
Adam: War "games"?

Chapter 11

Irritation.

Jane: This is a real test.
Adam: I am fully aware of that sir, but that doesn't mean it can't be fun.

Adam and Riley gear up. Scythe grabs an assault rifle off the wall. He tossed Blake a pistol.

Blake: I don't even know how to use this.
Scythe: Hopefully you won't have to.

Blake holsters the pistol. Riley takes two axes off the wall. They are entirely black with a glossy finish over them. They blur as he swings them through the air.

Riley: Good weight and balance to them.

The axes glow and disappear.

Riley: Ready.

Riley steps to the middle of the room. Scythe stands next to him. Blake stares at the wall of weapons in front of him.

Adam: Overwhelming huh?

Adam grabs a pistol, a rifle, and two knives.

Blake: Don't even know what I'm looking for.
Adam: Rifle and two sticks should work for you.
Blake: Thanks. So you aren't mad at me?

Adam: Why what'd you do?
Blake: (Smirks) I went against direct orders to save Scythe.
Adam: Seem like stupid orders in the first place.
Blake: Thanks.
Adam: Let's slaughter them!
Blake: Heck yes!

Blake and Adam walk to the center of the room.

Scythe: We are all very close combat specialized. Do what you can to get them close to you or someone else.

Everyone nods. An orb floats up from the floor. Scythe, Riley, and Adam place their hands on the orb. Blake follows. *Vmmmm!* They are transported to a concrete building. A glowing manila folder sits on the floor.

Adam: Nice, defending.
Scythe: I hate defending.
Blake: What are we defending?
Scythe: There is a word in that folder. If they say the word they win.
Blake: So we have to stop them from seeing it?
Scythe: That is correct.
Blake: That seems easy, which means it will be insanely difficult.
Scythe: Bingo. Riley and Blake you guard outside.
Riley: Yes sir.
Adam: Wait!
Scythe: What?
Adam: We need to decide on our team name. I vote dragons.

Chapter 11

Riley: An extinct arrogant reptile? No thanks.
Adam: Would you rather be the fluffy bunnies?
Riley: Anything is better than dragons.

Adam holds his arm out. Scythe puts his hand on Adam's hand. Riley and Blake follow suit. Excitement fills the small room.

Adam: Go team fluffy bunnies!

Disappointment fills the room.

Scythe: Really?
Adam: What?
Scythe: (Smirks) Remind me never to let you pick our name again.

Scythe touches his face and a white skull covers it. Adam touches his and a rabbit's face covers his. The nose is even twitching.

Blake: Wow, how do you do that?
Riley: Scythe is an agent so his mask is custom. Adam's... He obviously planned for us to be the fluffy bunnies from the start.
Adam: Why would I do that? Isn't it cute though!?

Riley touches his face and a blue shield covers his face. Blake touches his and his vison has a black tint to it.

Blake: So mine's black?
Scythe: Yep. Now get going.

Feelings of Power

They step out into a post-apocalyptic city. Random cars parked on the street and abandoned. The surrounding buildings have huge holes littering them. The sky is dark and filled with smoke.

Blake: What is this place?
Riley: This is where we do the field test. Anything other than that, you'll have to ask Scythe.
Blake: So you mad at me?
Riley: You had a good reason, probably should've kept your nose out of the Director's business.
Blake: Won't be doing that again.
Riley: Other than that, you got my field test day pushed up, so I am grateful.
Blake: Let's earn you some points.
Riley: Let's keep you with us.

They bump fists and focus on the street ahead.

Voice: Test commencing in 3...2...1...

BEEEP! A loud beep echoes through the empty streets.

Exhilaration. Excitement. Fear.

Blake points in the direction of the feelings.

Blake: Three coming this way.

Excitement isn't moving smoothly. They are way ahead of the other two.

Blake sees someone on top of a one story building for

Chapter 11

a split second. *Vmm!* They are directly in front of him with a knife. *Baboom!* His fist connects with their chest and they fly into the street.

Exhilaration and Surprise.

Exhilaration is on the roof with three very thin mannequins. They snap their fingers and the mannequins advance towards Riley and Blake. Each of the mannequins is dual-wielding swords. Blake holds up his rifle. *Crack! Crack!* He fires two shots that shatter the face of one of the mannequins. The remaining two cover ground quickly. *Shing!* One cuts Blake's gun in half. He jumps back and pulls out his two sticks. He doesn't have time to stop dodging. The mannequin's blades are going right for his heart. He continually backs up until... *Thud!* His back is against the wall. A blade grazes his shoulder and blood runs down his armor.

My only hope is to tackle this thing and crush it with Scythe's strength.

The world around him slows as he presses forward. The sounds of a clay pot breaking fills his ears. Amazingly he is about twenty feet away from the building. The controller of the mannequins now resides by their friend in the street.

Shock. Shock. Shock. Anger.

Riley removes the arms of his mannequin with a swing from each ax. And removes its head with a third swing. *Boom! Boom! Boom!* Dust and debris are flying up from a nearby building. *Boom!* A glowing form bursts onto the street. It stands in front of the other two and runs at Blake. Adrenaline fills Blake's veins as he charges back. Riley runs at the other two on the street. The glowing person jumps up. Blake slides underneath them. Blake jumps up and waits. They turn and look at him.

Looks like a female form. She also feels familiar.

She tries to grab Blake and he blocks and tries to grab her. *Boom!* Their fists collide and they are both thrown back.

That felt like hitting a brick wall.

Blake: I have this thing about hitting girls.
Glowing girl: Get over it.

She picks up a car and throws it at him. He catches it with one hand and throws it back. Riley jumps next to him.

Riley: We got this buddy.

Blake punches Riley in the chest and sends him flying.

Riley: Knew that wasn't me huh?
Blake: He said buddy.

Riley laughs and they square up to the glowing girl. A taller person walks up and stands next to her.

Glowing girl: About time you got here Lucas.

Chapter 11

Lucas: Not my fault you've been underestimating your opponents Victoria.

Victoria clenches her fists.

Victoria: I wasn't expecting them to clear through our friends so quickly.
Lucas: Overconfidence is quite the killer, but we can still pull off a win here. I'll take out blue, you take out black.
Victoria: I got this.

Lucas squares off with Riley. Riley charges and cuts him in half. Lucas vanishes. *Bang!* A shot fires from the roof and hits Riley in the right shoulder. Blake jumps over and grabs Riley. He brings him behind a car and into the building.

Scythe: He still alive?
Blake: Yeah, but I gotta get back out there before they charge in.
Scythe: I'll join you.
Blake: You sure?
Scythe: I'm getting cooped up in here.
Blake: Where's Adam?

Bang! A shot goes off on top of their building.

Adam: He's not on the roof anymore.

Scythe and Blake walk out. Lucas is standing next to Victoria holding his right shoulder.

Scythe: Wasn't expecting to see you out here Predator.
Lucas: Looks like rumors of your death were exaggerated as always.
Scythe: Death and I are good friends.
Lucas: Glad you aren't getting better acquainted.

Victoria charges at Blake. Scythe steps in and punches her in the gut. She flies and skips across the pavement.

Scythe: It's rude to interrupt. Got her?
Blake: Not much left to get after that.

Lucas and Scythe walk up to each other and shake hands.

Scythe: No holding back?

Lucas steps back.

Lucas: You know it.

Ten images of Lucas appear around Scythe. Blake sits on a car and keeps Victoria in his peripheral vision. Each Lucas pulls out a knife in unison.

Lucas: Now which one am I?
Blake: 3 o'clock?

Boom! Lucas flies into the car next to Blake.

Scythe: Good job. Thanks.
Blake: No problem.
Scythe: I'll make sure they don't get the folder.

Chapter 11

Blake: I'll do my best to take care of her.

Blake walks over to Victoria and takes a deep breath. Victoria is breathing heavily on all fours. She struggles to her feet. The glowing aura around her is cracked around her chest.

Blake: Do you give up?
Victoria: You cocky jerk.
Blake: I'm not cocky, I just prefer to not beat someone who is already down.

Victoria clenches her fists and the cracks vanish in her aura. She jumps up and brings both fists down on Blake. *Baboom!* He punches her in the stomach and she crashes into a building. Her glowing aura shatters and she falls to the ground. Blake runs over and picks her up.

Voice: Winner of round, fluffy bunnies. All opposition eliminated. Fifteen minutes until next round.
Blake: Are they serious?
Scythe: Let's get moving.

Blake and Scythe walk into the room with Riley and Adam.

Riley: Not going to lie, that was kind of easy.
Adam: You had to say it.
Riley: What?
Adam: We are so screwed now.
Riley: Sorry.

They appear in a weapons room again. Thane is waiting for them.

Thane: Good job.
Blake: (Smiles) Thanks.
Scythe: Get ready for the next round.

Thane walks up and inspects Blake's injured arm.

Blake: Forgot that thing sliced me.
Thane: It didn't, it only felt like it did.

Thane takes a picture with his tablet and shows Blake. There is a cut in the armor, but it doesn't go to the skin.

Thane: The pain was transferred to the nearby cells. There is also simulated blood in each layer of the suit.
Blake: Wow.

Thane uses a bright blue light on the suit and it looks good as new.

Blake: So Riley's shoulder?
Thane: Equally fine.

Thane walks over and repairs Riley's shoulder. Adam stands in the middle of the room.

Scythe: What's up?
Adam: Nothing, I just used one bullet so I'm pretty easy to reload.
Scythe: Gotcha.

Chapter 11

Blake takes a rifle off the wall and stands next to Adam.

Blake: Left mine back there.
Adam: Littering is bad Blake.
Blake: Oh sorry.

Blake's vision blurs. He shakes his head.

Adam: You alright?
Blake: Yeah, just a tired.
Adam: I saw you warp, that was cool.
Blake: Didn't do it intentionally, it just kind of happened.
Scythe: Combined with my ability, it made you into quite the wrecking ball.
Blake: No doubt about that.

Riley whips his axes around.

Riley: Doesn't it take a lot out of you to do that?

Yeah.

Blake: Not really.
Riley: Well it's amazing.

Scythe holds out his arm.

Scythe: Go team fluffy bunnies.

Amusement. Joy.

Blake, Riley, and Adam put out their arms.

In unison: Fluffy bunnies!

They are teleported back to the apocalyptic town. They appear on a street in a much different part of the city.

Scythe: Looks like we are on the attack.
Adam: Now we just have to find them.

Blake feels anticipation and points.

Blake: Over there.
Adam: Your ability seems kind of like cheating.
Scythe: Blake and Adam, take them straight on. Riley on the right flank. I'll take the left.
Adam: 10-4.
Blake: So we have to collect the folder and say the phrase?
Scythe: Yep.
Blake: Let's move.

Everyone starts running to the objective. *Ratatata!* Rapid fire rains down on them.

Pain.

Both Blake and Adam jump behind a car. Adam is holding his leg.

Adam: How did he get here so fast?
Blake: The flying probably helped?

Chapter 11

The person in question is flying toward them a couple hundred feet in the air.

Adam: Can you do that?
Blake: Nope.
Adam: He's not using wings, it has to be an ability.
Blake: Can't.
Adam: You afraid of heights?
Blake: Big 10-4 on that.

Blake turns and puts his hands under the car. He lifts and it doesn't budge.

Blake: Scythe is too far away.
Adam: Time for good old fashioned "put a lot of bullets in the air".

Adam stands up and rips fire into the air.

Pain and Fear.

The flying person rolls and lands behind a car about a hundred feet away.

Amusement.

Adam: Winged him.

Blake laughs.

Blake: You're terrible.
Adam: Yes I am.

Adam pulls out his knife and sticks Blake in the leg.

Blake: Ouch.
Adam: I'm going to keep doing that until you go get him.

Blake levitates off the ground slightly.

Blake: I hate you.
Adam: Go get him birdie.

Blake jumps and flies over the car very quickly. He stays close to the ground and lands on the hood of the car the flyer is hiding behind. He pulls out a stick and swings it.

Pain and Surprise.

The flyer jumps back a bit and pulls out a pistol. Blake jumps behind the car. The flyer jumps and flies away. Blake walks back to the car and grabs Adam.

Adam: Let's get him.

Blake shakes his head and grabs Adam by the vest. They head in the same direction as the flyer. Adam's feet drag on the ground.

Adam: A little higher?
Blake: Nope, pick up your legs.
Adam: Pansy.

Blake stops and they duck into a nearby gas station.

Chapter 11

Blake: That's fair.
Adam: I'm going to kill Riley.

They look at the building they have to infiltrate. It is an old police station with bars on the windows. A large person is standing in the doorway. The flyer is nowhere to be seen. The large person points at Blake and Adam's building.

Adam: Hooray, they know we're in here.

CHAPTER 12

Boom! The concrete wall in front of them explodes inward.

A large metal man crashes into Blake and Adam's building. He swings his arms and Blake and Adam barely dodge it. Blake feels something. He steps in front of the metal man. The man brings down both of his arms down on Blake. *Thud!* He catches the man's arms with his left forearm. *Boom!* He sends the man flying with his right fist.

Large man: Scythe is nearby.

Blake runs at full speed towards the large man. He jumps and his fist connects with the man's chest. *TUNG!!!* A metal vibration throws Blake back. Scythe catches him.

Scythe: Dan, can't say I expected you to be here.
Dan: My Junior agents are smarter than yours.

Chapter 12

Scythe: Because they picked a Second in Command that rarely sees the field over a Field Agent who fights every day?
Dan: Good to see you are healthy again, I won't be going easy on you.
Scythe: I can see that, you ok Blake?

Blood drips off of Blake's right hand.

Blake: Feels like I punched a tank.
Scythe: That'll happen, let's get him.
Dan: Olivia and Reggie, let's get going.

A feminine figure steps out of the Police Station. The metal man stands up and brushes himself off.

Scythe: Blake take the golem and watch out for the girl.
Blake: Golem?

Scythe dodges a rock Dan whips at him.

Scythe: The big metal guy.
Blake: Gotcha.

Blake charges at the golem. Olivia jumps in the way. Blake swings to knock her out of the way. His arm goes through her and she punches him in the gut. He swings again. His arm goes through her again and she punches him in the face. He takes a step back. The golem runs and jumps at him. Blake barely dodges and jumps further back. Blake charges the girl. The golem stands in front of him. Blake shoves it back and the girl appears through the golem. *Squish!* Adam sticks a knife in her side. She falls back. *Ratatata!* The flyer shoots and rips up Adam's left side. Blake grabs Adam and tosses him back into the gas station. *BOOM! BOOM! BOOM!* Dan and Scythe punch each other with enough force to shake the ground around them. *Boom!* Scythe pushes Dan into the Police Station. He dives behind the golem as bullets come his way. The bullets bounce off of the golem. He reaches over and grabs the girl lying on the ground. He throws her at the flyer. *Boom!* He punches the golem on top of Dan. The flyer catches the girl. *Bang! Bang!* Two shots each hit the flyer and the girl in the head. They fall to the ground. Blake jumps and catches them.

Adam: Only have one arm left, but that's all I need!

Dan picks the golem off of him and sets it down. He runs at Blake. Blake barely dodges. He pulls out his sticks and unleashes them on Dan rapidly. They snap and fall apart.

Amusement.

Dan smacks Blake and sends him flying. Blake catches himself on a nearby building and rockets at Dan. *Tung!* He crashes into the golem and the golem grabs him. Blake struggles to stop from being crushed. Scythe jumps in and rips the golem's arms off. *TUNG!* Dan punches Scythe in the face and sends him into the ground. *Carack! Boom!* Lightning hits Dan from the side and sends him flying.

Chapter 12

Riley: Get that folder!

Blake crawls his way into the police station.

Voice: Round over. Winner fluffy bunnies. Next round in one hour.

Riley, Adam, Scythe, and Blake appear in their weapon room.

Riley: How did you get it so quick?
Blake: I didn't.
Adam: One handed baby! No one pays attention to the crawling guy.
Blake: Are you ok Scythe?
Scythe: This suit is ridiculous, it paralyzed me from a weak hit like that.
Blake: What is Dan's ability?
Scythe: No clue.
Riley: What was their last person?
Adam: A guy really good at taking six shots in the back?
Blake: (Laughs) really?
Adam: He was itching to get out and fight. I got behind him, and I took him out.
Blake: That is perseverance.
Adam: Just glad I get to have all my limbs next round.
Blake: What is the next round?
Scythe: No clue, they don't usually go up to three rounds.

Jane: Forty five minutes ladies, better get ready.

Blake lays down on a bench and closes his eyes. He closes out the world around him and relaxes.

Voice: Five minutes to final match.

Blake jumps up. Riley, Scythe, and Adam do the same.

Blake: You all napped too?
Scythe: It was a good idea.
Adam: I just laid there to be part of the group.
Riley: I forgot you don't sleep.
Adam: Nope.
Scythe: Alright, we almost got slaughtered last time, we need to be more careful this time.
Riley: Agreed.

They are teleported back to the apocalyptic town. Blake notices the building they defended in round 1.

Blake: Defense again?
Scythe: Seems redundant.
Voice: Round three. Eliminate opposing forces.
Blake: Who are the opposing forces?
Scythe: You tell us.

Blake closes his eyes and feels around. He levitates slightly and warps forward.

Blake: Looks like both of them.

He smells the scent of wet dog.

Chapter 12

Weird.

Riley: Dan is obviously a priority to take out.
Scythe: If the other team knows that they will help us out.
Riley: Or they'll wait til he takes us out.
Scythe: That's more likely. Let's get to better cover.

They run into the next street and find a building with minimal damage.

Intense rage.

Blake looks out the window and see Victoria fighting Dan. She is swinging wildly and unfocused. *Boom!* Dan backhands her into the ground.

Blake: Found Dan.

Blake bolts out of the house and tackles Dan. Dan throws him off and jumps up. Blake walks over to Victoria. He still feels intense rage off of her.

Voice: I'll get him too.

A figure steps out and stares at Blake.

Blake: Ok?
Figure: Ok, he's immune.
Dan: Help the others.
Figure: Yes sir.

Victoria stands up. The glowing is cracked around her face.

Victoria: I don't need your help.
Blake: Well I need yours.

Dan jumps in and brings down both of his fists on Blake. Blake throws up both of his arms and closes his eyes. Dan jumps back. A glowing light wraps around Blake's entire body.

Victoria: How?
Blake: Told you I needed your help.

The cracks around Victoria's face vanish. Dan smashes the ground and kicks up dust everywhere. Blake charges right at him. *Tung! Tung! Tung!* He punches Dan multiple times. His last punch goes right through Dan. *BAM!* He is thrown by the golem.

Victoria: Olivia.

Vmm! Dan appears next to Victoria and Blake.

Victoria: Thanks Tim.

Blake warps in and punches Dan in the stomach. The world begins to spin around Blake.

This isn't good.

Chapter 12

Dan grabs Blake by the throat. The light around Blake's throat begins to crack. *Tung! Tung! Tung!* Victoria beats on Dan to no avail. Blake looks down at Dan's left hand. He is holding a chunk of metal. Blake kicks Dan's left hand as hard as he can. Dan's grip weakens and Victoria's next punch sends Dan to the ground. Blake jumps back and holds his neck. Victoria kicks Dan in the side. *Tunk!* She hits something hard and jumps back. The flyer picks up Dan and they fly off. Two figures covered completely in white appear between Victoria and Blake. One is holding a gladius and the other is cracking their knuckles. Adam jumps in front of Blake. Riley jumps in front of Victoria.

Blake: Who are these guys?
Riley: Team 4.

Adam spins his knives in his hands. Adam attacks the one with the gladius with blinding speed. They use the sword to deflect the knives quickly and quickly counterattack. Adam dodges and returns to fighting as close as possible. Riley swings his axes and his opponent dodges with no effort. A clawed hand goes for his chest. *Ting!* Victoria blocks it. *Bam!* She punches Riley's opponent in the face. *Squish! Squish!* Adam's daggers sink into each of his opponent shoulders. *TING!* Blake barely stops the gladius from cutting Adam in two. *Bang! Bang! Bang!* Adam fires six shots into the swordsman's chest. They step back for only a moment. Blake grabs their arm and head and begin to squeeze.

Blake: Give up Scipio!
Scipio: If you know who I am, you know I cannot.

Scipio grabs Blake with his free hand and pulls him off his back. *THUD!* Blake is thrown onto the ground hard. *Squish!* Blake is stabbed through the heart.

Riley: Blake!

Electricity wraps around Riley's hands. *BOOM!* His opponent is hit point blank and thrown into a concrete wall. Their armor turns black. Riley falls to his hands and knees. Adam blurs next to Scipio and grabs both knives from his shoulders. He tackles Scipio to the ground and rips the sword from Blake's chest. *Sching!* He runs the blade across Scipio's neck. Scipio's armor turns black. Adam runs over to Blake.

Adam: Wake up!

Blake snaps up and begins breathing heavily.

Riley: How did you survive that?

Victoria falls to her knees.

Blake: I'm assuming... I have no idea.

Blake continues to breathing heavily. *BOOM!* A large object lands about twenty feet from Blake. Scythe crawls out from the crater he left in the ground. He cracks his neck and walks back towards where he came from. Blake jumps up and follows Scythe. A tall man with a huge tower shield stands in their makeshift base.

Blake: What is he?

Chapter 12

Scythe: Lucas' brother. Feels no pain and almost as strong as I am. We call him Destroyer.
Destroyer: Almost as strong as you? I must've hit you pretty hard in the head for you to believe that.

Destroyer charges at Scythe and Scythe catches the shield. Destroyer pushes him into the wall. Scythe moves through the shield and Destroyer. *BAM!* Scythe hits Destroyer in the back of the head. His armor turns black.

Voice: Opposition defeated, round over. End of rounds. All points are being calculated.

Scythe: Thanks Olivia.

Olivia nods. Everyone is teleported into a large white room.

Director: Now that was a show. I want to thank Kylie, Scipio, and Isiah for being the opposition for this test.
Lucas: You have to go after me first Isiah?
Isiah: I smash who I see.
Director: Now you all did very well. I also awarded bonus points to those that ended fights as quickly as possible or helped to stop a prolonged battle.
Voice: Agent status achieved by the following. Victoria of Section 3. Sally of Section 3. Olivia of Section 2. Garret of Section 2. Adam of Section 1. Riley of Section 1. Blake of Section 1. Thank you all for participating.

Disappointment and Joy fills the room.

Director: Actually you will remain a Junior Agent Blake. The system is not usually used for this type of trial.
Blake: So I would've made it if this was the real test.
Director: Yes you would've. You actually scored more points than almost all the other applicants.
Blake: Can you tell me who beat me?
Director: Adam obtained the most points.
Blake: I can handle that.
Director: Shall we keep our noses on our faces from now on?
Blake: Yes sir.
Victoria: Sir, may I speak freely?
Director: And politely yes.
Victoria: Blake is as scary as they come.
Olivia: Seconded.
Riley: Agreed.
Dan: No doubt.
Director: So you would like to count this as a pass for his field agent test?
Dan: Yeah.
Director: I will take it highly into consideration.
Dan: Thank you sir.
Director: I want to thank you all for participating. You will resume normal duties tomorrow. Those of you that achieved Agent status will be briefed in the morning.

The Director walks up to Blake and places his hand on Blake's shoulder.

Director: You are most impressive, I want you to keep up the good work.
Blake: I will do my best.

Chapter 12

Director: Your pet has been freed and you can return home whenever you would like.
Blake: Thank you sir.

The Director smiles and walks out of the room. Blake snaps his fingers. Gauge appears next to him.

Blake: Long time no see bud.
Victoria: Is that a Demon Dog?
Blake: Yeah this is Gauge.

Blake pets him and Gauge wags his tail.

Victoria: Why didn't you use him out there?
Blake: I don't want him getting hurt.
Victoria: He's huge.
Blake: (laughs) Yeah he is.
Victoria: He better be out there next time.
Blake: We'll see.

Olivia comes up and walks away with Victoria. Riley walks up and pets Gauge.

Riley: Nice work out there.
Blake: Lightning?
Riley: Yeah, every Sorcerer of Battle needs a ranged move, lightning is mine.
Blake: That is wicked.
Adam: Well I will see you losers later. I'm going to see if this Agent status can get me a bigger budget in the garage.
Blake: Thanks for coming out Adam.
Adam: It was fun. Fluffy Bunnies forever!

Blake and Riley laugh. Scythe walks up and pets Gauge.

Scythe: Congrats Riley.
Riley: Thanks Scythe.
Scythe: Back to school tomorrow.
Blake: Yes, I'll be thankful for a little normal.
Scythe: Oh come on, that was fun.
Blake: Yeah it was, but it's a lot to take in all at once.
Scythe: Maybe they'll put you and Pulse on better missions now that they've seen what you can do.
Blake: We'll see.

Blake feels a warm feeling from behind him. Danielle wraps her arms around him.

Danielle: Good job.
Blake: Thanks.

Anger.

She punches him in the stomach.

Danielle: You going to be stupid like that again?
Blake: (Wincing) No.
Danielle: Good. I expect a good date tomorrow for all the worrying you made me do.
Blake: Consider it done.
Danielle: (Smiles) I'll see you tomorrow.

Danielle leaves. Blake notices a young boy standing by himself. He walks over to him.

Blake: Hi I'm Blake.

Chapter 12

Boy: I'm Perry.
Blake: I don't remember seeing you out there.
Perry: You saw my golem. I stay away from battle as much as possible.
Blake: I gotcha. Does he act on his own?
Perry: Kind of. Block knows how to defend himself, but takes orders from me.
Blake: Block? I like the name.
Perry: Thanks. He wasn't able to get me to the Agent status, so I will have to build him better.
Blake: How old are you?
Perry: Thirteen.
Blake: You have time.
Perry: The youngest agent ever was fifteen. I have two more years to make him tough enough for me to get in.
Blake: Best of luck.
Perry: Thank you.

Arms wrap around him but it doesn't give him a warm tingly feeling. They are also around his neck.

Pulse: Way to be kid.
Scythe: How's it going?
Pulse: Good. I'm supposed to take Blake home.
Scythe: About time, he deserves a better bed than a prison cell.
Pulse: Agreed.
Blake: So you're not mad at me?
Pulse: We were all pissed that you did what we couldn't. Not to mention you make us like you and then go try to die.
Blake: It wasn't on purpose.
Pulse: Let's have Sara check you out.

Blake: Or not?
Sara: I knew he would say that.
Blake: When did you get here?
Sara: Been watching the fights just like everyone else. Let's go.
Blake: Ugh…

Blake is taken to the office and lays down on a bed. Sara pulls out a scalpel.

Blake: Don't touch me with that!?
Sara: Shut it.

She cuts the suit down the middle and pulls it off of him.

Sara: So how did it feel to get stabbed in the heart?
Blake: Like someone ripped my chest out.
Sara: Sounds about right. How are you feeling besides that?
Blake: Really tired.
Sara: How many different people were you connected to at once?
Blake: Maybe five, I don't know, I was just trying to win.
Sara: You need to be more careful.
Blake: I will try.

Anger.

Sara grabs him by the throat and pins him to the bed.

Sara: These people do not care if you max yourself out! They simply care if you take out as many bad people as you can before you die.

Chapter 12

Blake: That voice sounds familiar.

Sara gets a blank expression on her face and her arms fall to her sides.

Sara: So how many people do you think you connected to at once?
Blake: Like three or four.
Sara: And how did you feel?
Blake: A little stressed but it didn't hurt me too bad.
Sara: Well your vitals appear to be holding strong. That doesn't mean "let's see if we can get our vitals worse". I'm just saying that you are holding up well.
Blake: I plan on taking it easy for a while.
Sara: That is good to hear. How'd the test go?
Blake: You didn't watch them?
Sara: I remember turning them on, but I must've fallen asleep.
Blake: What's the last thing you remember?
Sara: Turning the TV on. I don't even remember taking your suit off. I must need to rest.
Blake: Yeah, we both need some rest.
Sara: You could benefit from eating healthier.
Blake: Yeah, I supposed I could.
Sara: I'm just asking that you try.
Blake: I will.
Sara: Ok, everything looks good. You can go now.
Blake: I need clothes.
Sara: Oh they brought them over.

Blake gets dressed and heads out. Scythe and Grant are waiting for him. They jump in the car and head toward home.

Feelings of Power

Grant: You did awesome out there Blake.
Blake: It was fun.
Scythe: Think your dad will be happy to see me?
Blake: (Laughs) You are like my older brother. You might even be his favorite kid.
Scythe: Oh I doubt that.

Blake smiles and looks out the window as they drive. They arrive at home in no time. Rick is standing outside. Blake jumps out of the car and hugs him.

Rick: I'm assuming it went well?
Blake: All is good. Got a lot of compliments too.
Rick: That's good to hear. How are you feeling?
Blake: Like I got hit a lot by angry people.
Rick: Sounds like fun.

Scythe steps out of the car. Rick holds out his hand. Scythe shakes it.

Rick: Good to see you up and around.
Scythe: Good to be up and around.

They step into the house and Jeff yells.

Jeff: Good to see you guys.
Blake: Good to see you too Uncle Jeff.
Jeff: I ordered pizza because I'm too tired to cook. I've been worrying about you idiots.
Scythe: No need to worry about people as strong as us.
Blake: I believe you said something about being a friend of death?

Chapter 12

Scythe: More of acquaintances now, It's been a while since we hung out.

Blake steps outside.

Blake: Want to enjoy some pizza with us?
Grant: That actually sounds great.

Grant heads into the house. They enjoy their meal and Grant leaves. Blake lays down in his bed. *Snap!* Gauge appears next to his bed.

Blake: Happy to be back home?

Joy.

Blake: Me too.

Blake closes his eyes and the world goes dark.

Voice: It is very frustrating to protect you.
Blake: I don't need your protection.
Voice: You need it more than you think.
Blake: You are a disembodied voice, how are you protecting me.
Voice: This power of yours is meant for greater things.
Blake: Than helping people?
Voice: Humans have plenty of their own champions.
Blake: So am I a champion for the squirrels?
Voice: You are more powerful than they can control.
Blake: I'm more powerful than I can control!
Voice: You should not be putting yourself into these situations.

Blake: How else am I supposed to get better? All your words of wisdom do is get me frustrated.
Voice: Introduce light to someone who has been in the dark for so long and you are likely to blind them.
Blake: How about the tiniest amount of light? Like, who are you?
Voice: You wouldn't believe me if I told you.
Blake: Try me.
Voice: Why do you not ask this much of those around you?
Blake: Maybe because they tell me more than you ever have.

Silence.

Blake: Hooray, back to sleeping.

Blake awakes in the morning and pets Gauge. He steps into the living room/kitchen. Rick is standing by himself.

Worry and Fear.

Blake: Where are Scythe and Jeff?
Rick: Remember the conversation I wasn't ready to have?
Blake: Yeah.
Rick: We need to talk.